Knights Of The Blood

Blood

Kingdom Of Ash & Sorrow Book 1

by Arthur Drake

Table Of Contents

Newsletter

Arthur Drake here.

I wanted to let you know that you can get a free book by signing up to my newsletter below.

There, you'll receive updates on the latest books I'm working on, deals, discussions of horror novels, life in general, and a whole lot more.

Click the link below to sign up.

https://www.arthurdrakefiction.com/newsletter-signup/

Chapter 1

The priests say love will defeat the demons, but then again, the priests have never seen what a demon can do to a grown warrior.

To a mother, that cherished you since you were born.

To a sister, who had yet to have her first child.

To a brother, who thought you were his world.

Nor to a father, you once thought invincible.

No, there are many things the priests do not know, and how to deal with the demons is one of them.

I looked up at the night sky and saw cracks traced across it. Streaks of hellish purple cut across the star speckled blackness.

A light breeze is blowing. Were it not for the evil in the sky, it would be a nice, wonderful night. I leaned against the wall overlooking the grove below. Inside, my wife sleeps, somewhere deeper in my house my boy is probably up, reading.

But I am here.

Staring at what I know will be my doom, will be the doom of us all.

"Alaric?"

A soft, sweet voice.

One that usually brings pleasure to my ears. But now there is nothing but fear gripping me.

"Alaric," she repeats, knowing I cannot ignore her for long.

I turned around and looked at Josephine, my wife, standing on the balcony, her white shift fluttering in the breeze. She wiped at her long brown hair that blew into her face then she walked towards me.

I knew she could see the fear in my eyes. Try as I might, it was hard to hide anything from this woman. She stopped by me and reached up a slender hand, running it along my cheek. She glanced past me at the sky, then back at me.

Already she knew what troubled me. She threw her arms around me. I pulled her close to me, squeezing her.

"It will be okay." Her voice was barely a whisper.

"How do you know that?"

My voice is ragged, far more than I had intended. Thoughts of my butchered family flooded my mind. Thoughts of the stark fear when I had first seen the demons.

"Things are different now. We have the council, we have their magic."

"I know."

I stroked her back. Her words ring true, but they do little to lessen the fear gnawing my innards out.

"When I last saw those cracks—"

"Shh…do not speak of such things."

She cuts off my train of thoughts, something I am grateful for. We rock back and forth, holding each other. The breeze is nice and gentle. I hear it rustling the trees below.

It's a few minutes before she speaks again.

"Things are different now, Alaric."

"I know." I say again.

And I know.

But that doesn't matter to my gut. We turn, so I am facing the sky again. I see the purple cracks. Flashes of what could be lighting shooting off inside them.

"Alaric."

Josephine pushes herself away and looks up at me, searching my eyes. It's then I realize I'm shaking. I gulp, my mouth dry. I force a smile and nod.

"I'm okay."

She shakes her head and buries it against my chest. I close my eyes, shutting out reality for a few moments. I hear quiet footsteps behind me. Even though I know he's there, I don't want him to see me like this.

"Father?"

A young boy's voice. One on the cusp of adulthood. I release my wife and turn to my son, hoping the fear and terror that grips me is not showing.

I must be strong, if only for his sake.

He takes a few steps out from the shadow of the house and stares at me. I smile and walk over to him. I reach out my hand and grab his shoulder.

"What are you doing up, boy?"

Thankfully, my voice doesn't crack. He looks up at me; he glances at my eyes, and I know he knows. His eyes wander to the night beyond, the one streaked with the demon light. He frowns and furrows his brow.

"You're worried about the cracks."

I laugh and grab his shoulder harder, shaking it back and forth.

"What are you talking about?"

He glances up at me. His eyes bore into my own. He knows I'm lying. My smile fades. He's so much like his mother, sometimes it scares me.

I cough to clear my throat.

"I am fine."

"I didn't ask if you were fine."

His eyes continue to bore, always searching. I nod.

"I know…but that's what concerns you. No?"

He nods.

I look up at the sky.

"Things are different now," he says.

"I know, Erwin."

He looks over at his mother, then back at me.

"The council."

"I know."

He nods. "Then you have nothing to worry about."

Finally, a slight smile spread across the boy's lips.

"Aren't you a smart one?"

I walk over to a bench and sit down. Josephine came and sat next to me. Erwin walked to the wall and leaned over, staring at the grove beyond.

"It's a pleasant night," he says.

"So, it is," I reply.

Something hits me then. My wife's head nuzzles against my neck, my boy looking out over our land, and the damned cracks in the sky. One crack streaks behind Erwin's head, like it's about to swallow him up, like it is about to engulf us all. Josephine must feel the stiffness in me. She reaches a hand over and takes my own.

"Peace, Alaric," Her voice low so Erwin cannot hear.

But the boy knows.

As does she.

As do I.

What I am looking at, the streaks in the night sky. They portend something and that something is not good. Old memories threaten to come bubbling up and tear apart whatever good I have in these moments with them.

A ravenous wolf is at the door.

And I don't know what to do.

I can't have this taken from me. No matter what. I must protect them. My hand flexes as if to grab a sword at my side. Though I abhor violence, I am never far from my weapon.

Josephine holds me tighter. I hang my head. No matter the gentle breeze, the cool night, the warmth of my wife, and my son's presence.

I cannot shake the darkness closing in.

And it will never relent.

Never.

Chapter 2

There was one other I trusted. One other would know what the cracks portended. Warin, my mentor knight, surrogate father, and leader of my company. I made the hike up to our headquarters. I trained a cadre of knights there during the first hour.

The sun rose over the hills in the distance when I walked into the grand halls. Usually this early, the place was quiet, almost like a church. However, as I arrived, I saw carts piled up outside, strings of horses and donkeys along the road.

Bernhardt, a fellow knight, stood outside the door shaking his head. I waved at him as I approached. He looked up. He frowned, something rare for him.

"What is it?" I asked.

"Not good," replied Bernhardt, walking down the few steps towards me. "Council is here."

A chill went up my spine.

"The council?"

Bernhardt nodded.

"Mmhmm. They're in there with Warin now."

I cursed under my breath. Of course they were here. Bernhardt leaned back and whistled.

"Glad I have door duty today."

I shook my head and walked into the building. The front contained a large central hall. The floor of polished stone and columns ran along the sides. It's a beautiful room, used primarily for greetings, as our training rooms are all in the back and rather harsh.

Dozens of people walked around, many in robes, many unfamiliar. I spotted another brother knight amid the throng. He wore his emblazoned tunic and tried to direct some of the mass.

I entered the crowd and pushed forward. I took a side hall and walked towards Warin's chamber. I noticed his door was cracked open, and I heard low voices coming from it. I walked up and knocked on the door. I peeked my head into the room.

I saw Warin.

He stood with his back to me, his grey hair hanging down his back. In front of him was a man I had never seen before, but by the purple robes he wore I could tell he was a member of the council.

The council man frowned at me. Warin turned around and saw me. He waved me in.

"Janius," said Warin. "This is Alaric, one of my knights."

Janus made a curt nod towards me but otherwise seemed annoyed by my presence.

"Hello, Janius," I said.

The man looked at Warin.

"What's going on out there?" I asked.

"I suspect you know something of it," replied Warin, his eyes soft. "I know you saw the cracks."

I nodded.

"That's what I wanted to figure out…"

I looked over at the council member. He stared at me as if expecting judgement. I held up my hand.

"I can talk later."

"Might as well speak now," said Warin.

Janius cleared his throat.

"Does the council fear what's happening out there?" I asked.

Janius' eyes widened. Maybe I was being bold, but I wanted an answer.

"There…are concerns, of course. But it's a temporary slip. We're as strong as ever."

It was obvious the man did not believe the words he said to me. I walked over, standing at an angle to Warin and the council member.

"What happened?"

Janius' eyes narrowed. "We don't know precisely. Only that…things went wrong. We're adjusting as we speak. That is what I told Warin here."

Warin clamped his hand on my shoulder.

"You don't have to worry, Alaric. Things are nothing like they were."

Janius nodded.

I nodded. Though I trusted Warin, his words did not comfort me, and the council was comprised of politicians, men who lied as a profession.

"I must be going. It was a pleasure speaking with you gentlemen."

Janius bowed and left the room. I watched him go then turned to Warin.

"Alaric," he said, holding up his hands.

"You know what these cracks portend. They've never experienced what they bring," I said.

Warin sighed and looked down. "The council was here during the attacks of your childhood."

I scoffed. "Yes, in sheltered homes. Behind walls."

Warin nodded, he wouldn't look at me.

"What are they going to do?" I asked.

"If anything happens. We'll fight the demons."

I slammed my hand against a nearby desk. "Fight them? Look what good that did to my people, people you civilized folk think the greatest fighters in the land. They met with the demons and were slaughtered because of it."

I balled up my fist.

"The demons thrive off violence. Fighting will lead to death. They must be contained."

Warin looked at me. I saw a softness in his eyes.

"I know. I know your pain," he said. "I still remember plucking you from that village."

"And I will forever be grateful for it."

"That's not what I mean." Warin waved me off. "I know your experience with the demons is…different than most."

I nodded. "An understatement if I ever heard one."

"What I'm saying." Warin stared at me. "Is that it will not be like then. Your people were fierce, yes. That's why the demons targeted them, but it will be different this time. We have walls, organization, and we know the enemy."

"We don't know them. If we did we would not be fighting."

"Alaric."

I turned.

Septus, another brother knight, stood at the door with an expectant look on his face.

I smiled. "I'm aware. I'll be right there."

"I'll have them go through their paces," said Septus.

"That is wise," I replied.

Septus nodded and left. I turned to Warin.

"Maybe we can talk more later."

Warin smiled. "We will."

I walked out of the room, feeling less reassured than I had when I walked in. As I made my way through the halls, I heard conversations all around. Whispers about what was out there, what it meant, what could be coming.

I knew something the rest of them didn't.

What was out there was a concept to them, something they understood only from books or lectures. Not something they had lived through. A heavy hand slapped my shoulder and spun me around.

I stared into familiar green eyes.

Fion.

Someone else who knew what the cracks meant.

"I know you've seen what's out there," said Fion.

He grabbed my shoulder and pushed me into a quiet side room. He glanced around, his long red hair flopping about as he did.

He stood a head taller than me and looked down.

"The cracks, Alaric…they've returned. What are we going to do?"

I held out my hands.

"Warin said not to worry. Not yet."

"Bah." Fion threw his hands out. "He's saying that because the council nitwit is here."

Fion shook his head.

His opinion of the council was even less than mine.

"They can't do it, Alaric. You know that."

I nodded.

"It's held so far," I said.

Fion looked over at me and shook his head. "You're a fool." He turned towards me and smiled. "But I know you're lying, so it's alright."

A horn sounded in the distance. The call to training.

Fion waved me off.

"Go ahead. I know you have important things to do."

"Always." I smiled and nodded to Fion.

"Fion, find yourself something to do. Otherwise, you're going to be sitting around and stewing all day. And when that happens, you're insufferable."

"Thanks, mate," replied Fion. "That's just what I need right now."

I laughed and walked out the door.

But the sick feeling kept churning in my stomach. All the people, the council man meeting with Warin, the cracks in the sky.

The council would swear they had it under control.

But I had my doubts

Chapter 3

"Thank you for taking me along for this."

I glanced over at Warin. He leaned forward, reins in his hand, as our wagon trundled along the cobbled stones.

Warin nodded, offering a smile.

"Of course."

I looked at the road. People pressed in close on either side of the busy street. All around us, tall buildings rose. Ahead of us was the council's chamber, a tall tower near the center of the city.

We arrived and our wagon was parked. We walked across the drawbridge, and we went inside. Once inside, they guided us to a room in the interior. Warin and I stood on a small walkway. Beyond us was a circular room filled with council members.

The lords and guardians of the city.

Or at least that's how they saw themselves.

"Warin and Alaric. Please step forward," said a voice from the dimly lit room.

A grey-haired man sat on a raised seat in the center of the circle. He wore purple robes and kept his hands folded in his lap. His name was Septimus, and he was the most powerful man in the city.

"Brother Warin. Brother Alaric," began Septimus, "We are honored to have you in our presence today."

I glanced around at the many faces around me, all stern, all lost in the shadows of the room. Septimus was the only face I could see.

"We have much to discuss," said Septimus. "And little time to do so. Warin, speak what you may."

"Thank you, your honor," said Warin, stepping in front of Septimus.

He glanced around the room, offering smiles to the darkened faces.

"Septimus, honored members of the council, just yesterday Council Member Torvald spoke with me and told me of developments regarding the cracks."

A murmur went through the gathered mass. Warin continued.

"I have a brother knight here, Alaric, who was with the Danius tribes when the demons first attacked. He was a refugee I plucked from there as a boy."

I noticed Septimus stared at me, sizing me up. My people had never been friendly with the council, the thought of us as barbarians. I wished Warin had not shared that part of my story, but I trusted he was leading to something.

"There is fear in his heart, as there is in mine. We have seen the destruction caused by the cracks, and we—"

"That was before our magic."

A voice spoke from somewhere in the darkness. Septimus held up a hand for order.

"Indeed. Warin. That was before we took control of the fallen world. Tell us, what relevance does this sad and true story have for us now?" Septimus raised an eyebrow.

"Of course," continued Warin. "We see the cracks and we know what they portend. If we don't restrain them, what will happen?"

"You doubt our power?" asked another faceless member.

"Of course not." Warin held up his hands, always the diplomat.

"But…we are dealing with strange forces. What I want to know is what should I and my knights do to prepare and if…"

Warin's voice trailed off.

"If what, Warin?" asked Septimus.

"If a breach is required."

Breach.

The word made my heart skip a few beats. I felt woozy. The world around me spun. I took a deep breath, trying to calm myself.

To breach was to die.

To breach was suicide.

To breach was the job of the knights.

"There will be no breach," said Septimus. "We have evolved far beyond such primitive and ineffective measures."

Warin nodded. "Good to hear, your honor."

Septimus waved a hand as if attempting to cast a spell over us.

"We have it under control, gentlemen. The cracks are here, yes. But they will not break. Our magic, our control, is too strong. Our knowledge is too deep. We have had a setback, but nothing more."

Septimus smiled.

"I understand your fear friends. I cannot imagine coming from the past you two have."

Septimus made a fist and held it aloft.

"You are strong, and I salute you."

We returned the salute.

"Now go in peace and know we have this under control. The cracks will recede, and you can forget the madness of breaching. Of this, you have our complete assurance."

Warin smiled and bowed.

"We thank you for your time."

I bowed.

They spoke lies. I knew it. I knew what I saw, and I knew what my gut told me. They were politicians not wanting to admit mistakes, not wanting to admit defeat.

But when it all failed, when it all came crashing down, it would not be their heads on the line.

It would be ours.

Their wives would not be widows, nor their sons and daughters fatherless.

They did not know the cost.

And never would.

I stared at Warin as we rode back to the countryside.

"They're lying, Warin," I said.

Warin nodded, staring at the road.

"What if it breaks, Warin? What if we're sent in—"

Warin held up a hand.

"There are troubles enough for the day, Alaric." He turned to me, smiling, like I was still the scared boy he had picked up so many years ago.

"Let us not fret today. The council has held the fallen world in check since you were young. Let's allow them to work and we will do what we must when the time comes."

I nodded.

Feeling sick.

Chapter 4

A few days later, I stood on a busy market street, my head dizzy. Erwin was off by a well, trying to impress some girls with some nonsense or another. Josephine stood at the stall to my right, turning over some ripened apples. She conversed with the shopkeeper about the origin of the apples, the conditions they grew in, the shopkeeper's personal preference for growing apples, and various other topics.

Usually, such a day would fill me with happiness. To get away from training and duty for a spell and enjoy the market. But today peace was far from my mind.

I turned over Septimus's words in my mind. From the start, I knew he was lying. I knew their feeble magic would not turn the cracks back.

I scratched my neck.

"Alaric."

Josephine's voice brought me away from my thoughts.

"Yes?" I asked, smiling.

She frowned, then smiled as she turned to the shopkeeper.

"This is Mildred. Her and her husband have kept an apple orchard over by Mt. Sinaus for three generations now."

"Three generations?" I asked.

I looked at the wizened woman and her applies. She smiled a toothless smile, her eyes lost amid her dimples.

I nodded to her.

"I'm sure they're delicious apples, madam."

She laughed.

"You have yourself a gentleman there," said the woman.

Josephine waved her hand. "Hah, you should see him at home. He is many things, but a gentleman I think not."

Josephine leaned into me, looking up into my eyes.

"But I love him."

She scooted up towards me. I leaned down and kissed her. The old lady cackled.

"You two will last long, I can tell."

"Thank you," replied Josephine.

I scanned the crowd. A habit I have. Constantly checking for signs of danger. The alertness is always there, like an animal. I glanced over and saw a dog sitting next to his owner. The owner haggled with a shopkeeper.

The dog's eyes flitted through the crowd. Identifying potential threats, potential meals, reading the signs of what was around him. The dog and I locked eyes for a moment. It might sound foolish, but I felt a moment of kinship there.

Then our eyes went back to roaming, looking for signs, always searching for signs. I spotted a stall further down. One made my heart leap a little.

It was a clothing stall, and hanging outside it, was a beautiful red cloak. One that looked eerily like one Josephine had lost last winter when I dragged her on a hunt. One she loved dearly. Josephine had grabbed her apples and looked at me.

I glanced at her and smiled.

She smiled back. "What is it? I saw that glint in your eye. What are you thinking about?"

I glanced over at Erwin, then shot through the crowd, snatching Josephine's hand and leading her behind me. She laughed as we parted through the crowd.

"Where are you taking me, sir knight?" she asked.

I pulled her in front of the shop and stood her before the cloak. I stepped back and threw my hands out as if presenting the cloak to an audience of hundreds. Josephine clapped a hand to her mouth.

She glanced at me, then back at the cloak.

"Alaric," she said, her voice hushed.

"I know it's not the one you had, but I figure it's something."

Her smile grew wider, then it turned into a frown.

"Alaric…we can't afford this."

"Stop."

I took two steps forward and placed my hands on her shoulders.

"Yes, we can. And we're going to get it. You're going to get it and you're going to wear it and you're going to love it."

She smiled and laughed. A few moments later, we walked down the street hand in hand. She with a thick red cloak on despite the spring heat.

"I love it," she said, running her hands over the material. "It's luxurious."

I laughed. "Luxurious, eh?"

She nodded and leaned against me. Erwin emerged from the crowd. He looked at his mother's dress, then at me.

"You do something wrong?"

"No boy," I said, reaching out and grabbing him. "Nothing at all."

He shrugged.

"Why don't we get something special for you while we're here," I said.

"You're being generous," said Josephine.

I shrugged. "Why not?"

I didn't want to tell them where it came from. Somewhere deep down, I had this nagging feeling something terrible was coming, something horrible was going to happen, and it would separate me from them forever.

"Alaric."

Worry laced Josephine's voice.

I looked at her and could already tell my face had changed. I smiled, but her suspicion was up. She glanced skyward where the cracks still shone, more dim in the day, but they were still there.

She squeezed my hand tighter.

"What about a practice sword, father, one of the wooden ones?" asked Erwin.

I frowned. "You know how I feel about such things."

He rolled his eyes and looked up at me. "But you're a knight! That's not fair."

"Boy, I did not choose this life and were it not for Warin, I'd leave this foolishness behind. But I owe him. Violence will never get you anywhere. Look what it did to—"

"I know." Erwin held up a hand. "You do not have to remind me."

"Sometimes I feel like I do."

A sense of sadness overwhelmed me. I wanted this to be a joyous occasion. I wanted to get something special for him, not fight with him.

"Let's find something else, though," I said, hoping to save the moment.

Erwin nodded. I could sense the specialness had vanished.

"There are many things you like, Erwin," said Josephine.

"I know," Erwin smiled. "We'll find something."

"That's my boy," I said.

I knew he didn't mean it, but I appreciated the attitude. I looked up to scan the stalls then froze in my tracks, yanking Josephine back as she tried to step forward.

"Alaric?"

I heard her but did not see her.

Fion was dressed in battle gear. He rode a warhorse and behind it was another. It's saddle empty. I saw the bag that hung off the horse's side and knew what it contained.

My armor.

"What's Fion doing here?" asked Erwin.

I heard notes of excitement in his voice, and it annoyed me.

"Stay here," I said, harsher than I meant to.

I released Josephine's hand and made my way to Fion. He looked grim atop his black horse. I walked up next to him. His eyes remained focused ahead, his red locks falling like dead leaves around his head.

I reached his side.

"What is it?"

"A call," said Fion.

My chest tightened.

"A call?"

Fion nodded once.

"To arms."

Sweat beaded my forehead and ripped down my neck. I reached up to steady myself against his horse and realized my hand shook.

"To arms…"

Fion nodded again.

"A village."

A village? Perhaps then, there was still some hope.

"There's been an attack."

My heart sunk again.

"An attack?" I asked.

"Yes." Fion looked over at me, his eyes dark. "Demons, they've broken through the cracks. An isolated incident, but we need to ride, save what we can."

Fion looked over at my family.

"You know what to do."

I did. I had to tell them goodbye and ride off. Because people needed me, and I was a knight.

I approached Josephine.

"Is it—"

"No," I said, pulling Josephine close.

It was just a call. Just a call to a village. Not the call I expected. Things could, would, still be fine.

I had to believe that.

For their sake.

For my own.

Chapter 5

Smoke rose from a grass-covered hill in front of us. We followed a winding road through acres of farmland. Ahead of us was Treve, a small village on the outskirts of the kingdom. I straightened on my horse.

No matter how many times I smelled the smoke, no matter how many times I saw the dying flames. My mind raced back to old memories. Of death, of destruction, of loss. I tightened my grip on the reins.

Once we were in the village, once the threat of demons was present and pressing, the old memories would wither, replaced by the sharp thoughts of survival.

But in the time in-between, they left me to sit with them and suffer.

We rounded the bend, and the village came into view. I frowned, stiffening at what I saw.

Men, women, children, animals. All torn apart and stretched. Staked up on pikes, stuck to walls, body parts missing and twisted. Warin rode at the fore. The sound of his sword being drawn from his sheath was like music to my ears.

I grabbed my sword, despite my distaste for the thing, and ripped it free. Battle meant freedom from thought, freedom from the memories of the past, if only for a few moments.

Survival pushed out everything non-essential. A natural bliss state, one I hated to admit I loved.

We rode forward, all yelling war cries. Our horses thundered under us. We rode forward to deliver justice, to spill blood, and to avenge the fallen.

We ran down the main street of the village, our eyes flicking to the left and right, expecting inhuman forms to leap out on us. We rode out to the other side of the village and took a wide turn, charging back in.

Warin pulled up his horse at the village center. His helm was down, and he snapped his head left and right. Like a cornered dog trying to find its attacker. He spun his horse around and faced us.

"Dismount."

I threw one leg over my horse and hit the ground, my armor shaking as I did. I slipped the visor over my eyes, blocking out the world beyond. Something I was grateful for.

I saw Fion and he saw me. We banded together and branched out from the main path. Our swords held taut.

I neared a decrepit hovel. The thatch on the roof had caved in and someone had broken through parts of the mud walls. A dead goat lay on the outside. Its neck twisted.

That was one other thing I hated about the demons. They not only slew and killed men, but also the animals, everything that revealed health, that revealed life.

I looked at the darkened interior of the hovel. A tattered curtain blew from an open window at the far side. Dark shapes lie on the floor. From their smell, I knew they were dead, likely desecrated, bodies.

I glanced at Fion, looking at his eyes through the slit in his helm. He gave a nod. We burst into the room with a yell, our swords held high, whirling this way and that. Ready to fight all the legions of hell together.

But the hovel was empty.

At least of demons.

I glanced down. A young girl lay at my feet. Her face showed disfigurement, and her body was charred. I looked up and saw two brothers closer to the door. One held a kitchen knife in a twisted arm, the other their mother's frying pan.

Pain had twisted both of their faces into grimaces. Their fate could not have been kind. My eyes flicked around the rest of the room, taking it all in, looking for signs, signs of the enemy, signs of the fight.

Like a dog.

The hovel was empty. Me and Fion filed out of the hut and back onto the street. We moved like two dancers in sync, like wolves in a pack. We tread down the street, our eyes searching the alleys and buildings on either side of the road. Other knights emerged from homes, their eyes hollow.

Feelings would come.

But not right now.

Later.

At night, in our dreams, when the faces of our wives and children turned to decaying bodies and spirits of death.

I saw a stack of men, all tied together, their faces twisted with agony, their lower halves burned. I saw a woman, her head caved in, leaning against a doorpost. Two infants lay dead before her, they had been trampled, their bodies mush.

We finished our patrol and met with Warin at the village entrance. His helm was off and cradled in the crook of his arm. He frowned and looked at the destruction around us. To his right was a house larger than the rest.

I walked towards it.

"Alaric," said Warin.

I ignored him and walked up the small stairs to get in. I pressed open the door and looked inside. At my feet was a man, the end of a broken spear in his hands. His face caved in. Behind him was a woman, a bloody knife a few paces from her broken body.

Beyond them was a boy, a javelin through his neck. No doubt one he tried to defend himself with. It was then the emotions came flooding in.

That wasn't supposed to happen, not yet.

The boy became Erwin, the woman, Josephine, and the dead man…

The man could do nothing to protect his family. The man could have been the greatest warrior in the world, but it didn't matter.

The man was me, and this was my family. I took a few stumbling steps back. Fion smacked a hand on my shoulder.

"Alright, Alaric," he said, in a voice so like a mother comforting her child.

The voice he used for when I was drunk or when he wanted me to know it was alright. That it was alright I couldn't take on the world, it was alright I was just a human.

Fion escorted me from the room and out to Warin. Warin talked with another knight. Their words came to me in a fuzzy echo.

I looked up. Warin glanced at me. He gave a quick frown, then returned to his conversation. The frown saying he told me so and I knew it.

I walked over to them, the fresh air helping me to stay on my feet. Warin turned to me.

"The council doesn't know what they're doing."

I blurted the words out, unsure exactly where they came from.

Warin's mouth opened, then closed. He looked at me for a moment, then continued.

"The demons have long moved on. We were too late. We'll have to send scouts in all directions. I doubt they can stay on this side long, but there are villages close enough they could be in danger."

Warin looked at Fion.

"Fion, I want you to scout Limren with Bartholomew."

Warin turned to the brother knight that spoke with him.

"Fredrick, you are to take Percy and head to Rivenwald. Quickly now."

Fion and Fredrick left, leaving Warin with me.

"They don't know what they're doing," I said.

"Alaric."

"They're lying." I took a step towards Warin, my voice low, tight.

"They're going to get people killed."

"Alaric…" Warin's eyes narrowed.

"They can't hold it back Warin. We're all doomed. The cracks are going to break and we're all going to die. I've seen I—"

"Brother Knight."

I quieted.

Warin saved his 'brother knights' for when we were severely out of line. Which I knew I was. I took a step back and hung my head. Shame crowding out my fear for a few moments.

"Forgive me."

Warin stepped close to me and placed a hand on my shoulder. He leaned in close.

"Things are not as we wish, Alaric. But you are a knight, and you must compose yourself like one."

"Yes, sir, of course, sir."

Alaric leaned his head against mine.

"The same fear beats in my heart."

He leaned back and sighed.

"The call will come," I said.

Warin looked down, not saying anything.

"They're not as powerful as they believe."

"We will do as we must, Alaric."

Warin looked me in the eye.

"What other choice is there? Give up and let the demons run roughshod over everything we value and love?"

"Of course not," I replied, anger burning in my heart.

Warin nodded.

"Then, like I said, we will do what we must."

Chapter 6

My heart was heavy as I rode towards my home. I crested a hill and saw it nestled below. Plains stretched out to the right, the tall grass waving, a few cattle dotting the landscape. To the right was the grove and beyond it, forested foothills that led to the mountains beyond.

I took a deep breath of fresh air.

I loved this place.

Smoke rose from our chimney, and I knew Josephine would be making something delicious, something intricate, something she had worked hard on.

Anything to distract her from me being at the front.

I kicked at my horse's sides, and we rushed down towards the villa. After sheltering the horse, I threw open the front door. Josephine spun around, her hair tied back and her hands still holding a cleaver.

She set the cleaver down and raced over to me. She threw her arms around me, and I spun her, setting her down. I heard thundering footsteps from the stairs above. I looked and saw Erwin rushing around the corner.

He stopped at the landing, his eyes widened as he saw me. Josephine stepped away as he rushed down and threw his arms around me. I grabbed him and squeezed him. Tears sprang to my eyes. I could not be happier than at that moment.

But I knew the demons were not done, and the council would not close the cracks.

I knew dark days were coming…and it was too much.

I started blubbering. Erwin stiffened in my arms. A white paleness draped itself across Josephine's features. She stood rigid as the tears flowed down my face. I don't know if Erwin had ever seen me cry and Josephine only had a handful of times.

I wiped my eyes, but the tears would not stop. Tilting my head back, I gazed at the ceiling. I closed my eyes tight and took a deep breath, trying to steady myself.

I felt Josephine's arms around me.

"Father?"

I looked down and saw Erwin had taken a step back, staring at me, concern etched into his face. I smiled and nodded.

"I'm sorry, son." I said, my voice soft. "I am okay. It has just been such a long journey.

Erwin nodded.

"Come on," said Josephine, whisking me towards the kitchen. "Have some food."

"What happened, father?" asked Erwin, tagging behind.

"Enough, Erwin. You know better," said Josephine.

"I'm sorry."

I turned to Erwin. "It's alright, we'll talk later."

He nodded. Josephine took me to our kitchen table and sat me down. She set a bowl of steaming, goodness before me. I engulfed it. I had not realized how hungry I was. Before I knew it, she had set a drink next to me.

I ate three rounds of the bowl and knocked down three cups of the drink. Then I sat back, feeling tired.

Erwin sat at the table, spooning some of the food into his mouth. Josephine sat down and ate her own.

"I failed them."

I spoke more to the room than to either of them. Erwin nearly dropped his spoon. Josephine glanced at Erwin, then back at me. Her eyes had that look.

She asked me if I meant to say this in front of the boy.

"He's old enough." I said, leaning forward, placing my elbows on the table.

"Who did you fail, father?" asked Erwin, his voice barely a whisper, like he was making a naughty joke instead of asking his father a question.

"The villagers I saw," I replied.

I gazed ahead. Right now, it was too much to look them in the eyes.

I held my head in my hands.

"I'm fine, I said. "It's just been a long journey."

"Then we'll get you to sleep," said Josephine.

That night I lay in bed staring out at the moonlit landscape beyond. The air was cool and pleasant, but sleep eluded me.

I heard Josephine stir beside me and looked over. She rolled over and opened her eyes.

"You're still awake," She said.

I nodded.

She slid up and nuzzled against me.

"Is there anything I can do?"

I shrugged. "No."

"Do you want to talk about what happened?"

I shrugged again.

"It wasn't what happened," I said.

"No?"

I shook my head, looking back out at the landscape, at the mountains in the distance.

"No. We found a sacked village."

"Like your own."

I nodded. "Like my own."

"And that brought up memories."

I shook my head. "No...well..." I sighed. "Yes. Ruined villages always do, but that wasn't it."

"No? So, what was it?"

"I..."

I looked back at her.

"The council doesn't have this under control. The cracks...they're getting stronger. There have already been incursions and..."

I grit my teeth. "I don't know."

"The council has closed them before," said Josephine.

"You're right but..."

I felt hot.

"I feel this time will be different. A village has already been sacked."

"Many were sacked before." Josephine sat up in the bed, clinging tight to me.

"That does not mean..."

"It might."

"No." Her voice was low.

I stood up and walked to the balcony, looking down at the grove below. She walked out next to me, interlacing her arm through mine.

"They did it once. They will not require…that, of you."

Breach.

The word kept flying around in my head ever since meeting with the council, like a trapped bird trying to get out.

"It is required of the knights."

"It has not been. Not since you were a boy."

I held up a hand to the night sky. The cracks laced through it, a few of them pulsed, growing bigger, longer.

"Help me, Josephine."

She held her head against my arm. I felt wetness.

I looked down and saw tears streaking down my arm. Her tears.

"Josephine," I said, feeling like an ass.

I turned her to me and pulled her in, holding her.

"I wish there was more I could do for you, Alaric. I wish I could take your pain myself."

"No," I said, rocking her back and forth. "I would not want that. I…I just fear what may come."

"I know, Alaric. I know."

Her soft sobs soon quieted. We stood holding each other.

After several minutes of silence, I spoke.

"Perhaps you're right."

She looked up at me, her hair matted against her face.

"You think so?"

"The council has handled this before, perhaps…perhaps that, will not be required."

The tension left her body. She threw her arms around me, squeezing tighter.

"I love you, Alaric."

"I know," I said. "I love you too."

I led Josephine back to bed. We slid in and she was soon asleep. I stared outside at the cracks.

I knew what was coming, what was inevitable. Despite what I tried to tell myself, what I tried to tell Josephine, the reality set in.

The knights would be required to breach.

Chapter 7

"Don't speak." Warin's voice was tight.

The wagon rattled us back and forth. The sky was dark, rain pattered across the city. I held a heavy cloak tight around me, the hood up.

I was exhausted. I barely slept the night before, nightmares of what lay beyond the cracks woke me every few hours.

Warin showed up and said we had to meet with the council. It had been less than a week since the village sacking, and something worse had happened.

I stared at the cobbles as the horses pulling the wagon clopped over them, at the rain wetting the stone and sliding into the divots.

I felt a hand on my shoulder and looked up. We were outside the council's chamber.

"Don't speak, not until the end," said Warin.

I nodded.

We got off the wagon and walked inside. Soon we stood before the council once more. I had trouble meeting their eyes. Septimus sat before us in his raised chair. I wanted to scream at him, ask him why they weren't doing more, if they were going to let their pride be responsible for more death. But I kept my mouth shut.

Septimus leaned forward, the chair creaked under his weight.

Warin stood up straight.

"What news, Septimus?" he asked.

Septimus looked aged, more than he had a week ago. He rubbed circles into his temple, his eyes red rimmed.

"Three more villages." Septimus hissed out the words.

"Three?" There was shock in Warin's voice.

Septimus nodded. "Three."

My heart sank. My hands shook, and my mouth felt dry. My heart pounded so loud I couldn't hear the next words. I looked up at Septimus. His mouth moved, but I couldn't make out what he said.

I turned to Warin. Warin had a frown etched onto his face, a rare occurrence. I took a few deep breaths and could hear again.

"Women, children, animals...we have seen all these before." Septimus spoke, "And after they go into the woods, they harm the animals, the trees, the water, everything they can touch."

Warin sighed.

"How soon until the cracks are closed?"

Septimus didn't answer. I turned to him, stared up at him. At the man that was supposed to solve all of this, the man that was supposed to have it under control.

The man clearly didn't.

"We are getting close..."

"Close?" asked Warin. "How close? What does that mean?"

Septimus closed his eyes and scratched his beard. I glanced around the council chamber. Though it was hard to see in the shadows, I saw fear etched into the faces there. They faced something they didn't know how to control, and it scared them.

"Septimus," said Warin.

Septimus threw out a hand. "We do not know. We have never dealt with something like this before."

But they had. Is that not what he had told us barely a week before? I bit my lip. I wanted to say something. I wanted to say many things. But none of them would help Warin find out information. None of them would change what was happening outside the high walls of the city.

"And that's not all…" Septimus looked like he was about to collapse.

"What else?" asked Warin.

"The cracks…more are opening. More are coming through and they're moving."

"Moving?"

Septimus nodded, not looking us in the eyes.

"They are moving closer and closer to populated areas."

"Damn…" Warin looked down, grabbing at his chin.

"If things keep up. It won't be long before they hit the city. And…" Septimus' voice trailed off.

Warin held up a hand. "We know how that would go. We do not need to speak of it."

Warin glanced over at me for a moment, then back to Septimus.

"So, what are we going to do to prevent this? To prevent any more loss of life?"

Septimus looked at Warin.

"We did not do this," said Septimus.

"I know."

"This is not our fault."

"Of course."

I cocked my head to the side, studying Septimus. What was he getting at? Why even bring that up? None of us thought it was his fault.

My next thought was it must be their fault. The council must have done something that brought the cracks back. I squeezed my hands into fists. I wanted to dig into Septimus, beat the details out of his pompous ass, about what went on in their closed chambers.

But I knew I'd never know.

We just had to deal with the consequences.

Silence reigned in the chamber for a few moments.

"What are we going to do?" asked Warin.

"I…" Septimus glanced around the room, as if seeking aid.

"We are working on it." A faceless voice spoke from the darkness.

"What is being done?" asked Warin, searching through the faces, looking for the source of the voice.

"We are doing our best," said Septimus.

"And the knights…what can we do?"

Septimus looked up, glancing around the room. My heart quickened. I knew what was coming.

If they didn't today, then they would tomorrow or a week from now. The words I feared to hear more than anything.

"We are addressing it," said Septimus. "You will continue your patrols. And…if we need you, we will send for you."

Warin nodded and bowed. "Very well. Thank you."

My hand clenched and unclenched around my sword pommel. I glanced over at Warin. He would not meet my eyes. He knew what he would see there, what I would ask. I looked at Septimus.

The council leader would not meet my eyes either.

I cleared my throat. Septimus looked at me.

A question burned on my tongue. I wanted an answer.

Had the magic failed? Had their magic failed?

But they would only interpret that one way. Their answer could only be no, for the council does not fail. I turned my head away and looked down. Warin gave me a look of approval.

"Is there anything else, dear knights?" asked Septimus.

"No," replied Warin. "Nothing at all."

Chapter 8

I had never seen Erwin so excited before. He bounced around on the balls of his feet, looking at what he held in his hands as if it was a sacred relic. He looked up at me, his eyes still wide with disbelief.

A smile threatened to split out the side of his face.

"This is not a joke?" he asked.

For the fifth time.

I shook my head. "No joke."

Erwin laughed and spun, like he was a five-year-old child again. Josephine looked at him out of the corner of my eye. She leaned against one of our apple trees, a hand held to her face, but the smile was still clear.

Erwin looked at me, looking me up and down.

"Well?" he asked.

I stood up from the rock I sat on and stretched.

"I don't know lad," I said, trying to hide my smile. "It's your first day, after all. Maybe I should find someone more your speed."

"Oh, enough." Erwin smiled as he swished his wooden practice sword through the air a few times. "Have at me."

He looked at me, his eyes glittered with joy.

I walked towards him real slow, glancing off towards his mother.

"I don't know, son." I flicked my hand out, using my practice sword to knock his own from his hands.

His sword fell to the ground.

"Are you sure you're ready?" I finished.

Erwin laughed and rushed for his sword. He grabbed it and squared off with me. We battled back and forth. I instructed him as we went. His stance, the way he struck, his defense, oh how his defense needed work.

We worked ourselves into a sweat and collapsed. Josephine brought us waterskins we downed. I looked over at Erwin. I had never seen such a contented look on the boy's face.

Part of it worried me. I wanted him to be as far away from violence and the love of violence as I could. I had never let him train with swords before. I had even kept him away from the wrestle box fields.

I knew he was mad about it, the hypocrisy of it all, but I was doing the best I could. I knew what such love wrought. I leaned back against the trunk of the apple tree, breathing in the fresh air of the grove.

Josephine crouched next to me. Erwin was up again and rushed away, his sword tucked into his belt.

Josephine looked at me. "He gets so much joy from it. Surely training in arms is not so bad?"

I frowned.

"He is not the ones you grew up with, Alaric. He will not let it lead him to pride."

"Violence leads to death. It begets death. Better for him to learn the art of speaking. That will get him further in this world."

Josephine frowned and looked at a dusty patch in the grove. What was coming weighed on her just as much as it did me. Despite the joy I was experiencing, the fear was never far away, nibbling at the edge. A wolf, ready to pounce.

"Such a nice day," said Josephine.

"Indeed, it is," I said. "And no better company." I yanked her against me.

Her voice caught, and then she relaxed. I could tell she was close to tears. My heart beat fast.

"Let's not let this moment be robbed of joy," I said.

She nodded against my chest.

"We'll do all we can to preserve what is good," I said. "And not let fear rob us of what we have."

"That is wise, husband."

We cradled each other as Erwin rushed about the grove, getting used to his new sword. Something caught his attention, and he rushed away. I looked over my shoulder but lost him among the trees.

Josephine and I sat down and relaxed against a tree.

I breathed out. Above, the sky was blue, filled with puffy clouds. The breeze was soft, the grove warm. I felt myself drift away when I heard the clop of horse hooves in the distance.

Alarm shot through my heart, and my eyes opened wide. My heart rate quickened. Josephine looked up. Her brow creased and worry lined her features.

I went to stand up. Josephine released me so I could. Erwin ran through the grove. He waved a hand over his head. I moved towards him.

"What is it?"

"Warin. Warin is riding here."

Erwin still smiled; no understanding of what Warin's visit could portend. I walked over to him and grabbed his shoulder as I passed.

"Is everything alright, father?" he asked.

I didn't have the heart to answer him truly.

"Go to your mother. I'll speak with Warin."

I walked out of the grove and down the path. There, like a dark knight from a fable, was Warin.

He sat atop his destrier, his armor on, and a grim look on his face. He was here to deliver news, news I would not want to hear.

I walked towards him. Feeling like a man walking to the gallows. I stopped a few paces from him and looked up.

I sighed.

He nodded.

"Word has come from the council."

His voice was tight.

"Another attack?" I asked. "Are we to ride out?"

He frowned. I saw a sparkle in his eye.

"If only."

My heart dropped. A yawning black pit had opened underneath my feet and swallowed me whole. I heard Warin as if he spoke from a great height above me.

"The council has called for a breach. The council chose three knights. You, me, and Fion. We—"

A great wave drowned out anything else Warin said. His lips moved but I heard nothing. The cracks behind him seemed to grow brighter as he finished his speech.

I shook my head.

"We're to...breach?"

He nodded once.

"You have a day to make well. Now I must continue my ride." Warin gave a nod and rode off.

As he left, I watched the dust his horse kicked up. He was off to shatter another man's hopes and dreams, off to make another mother cry.

I did not envy him.

I turned, and Josephine was there. Tears already streaked her face. Erwin stood a few paces behind her. He looked back and forth at us, worry on his face, trying to figure out what was going on.

She looked into my eyes. I nodded. Fresh sobs escaped her lips as she ran to me. She threw her arms around me. My arms hung at my side. Everything seemed far away.

I noticed it was dark; an approaching storm clouded the sky. Thunder rumbled.

Everything seemed like it was falling apart.

And I didn't know what to do.

Chapter 9

The next few hours passed in a haze. Josephine dried her tears and prepared a meal. A splendid meal she threw herself into. I walked with Erwin into the grove and tried my best to explain to him what was to come.

The boy was wise and seemed to grasp it right away. I saw pain on his face, but he did not cry in front of me. We sat that night around the dinner table and ate a grand meal in silence. After the meal, we all worked together to clean up.

I set a fire that night, despite the warmth outside. We all sat around and stared at it until the later hours. Erwin was first to go to sleep, then Josephine. Sleep eluded me as I knew it would.

I went to my study on the upper floor. A room filled with dusty old books and parchment scattered this way and that. A room where I did my best thinking, or so I thought.

I sat in that room, trying to compose a letter. Something to leave for Erwin and Josephine when I left, something for them to remember me by. The rising sun brightened my window before I had put anything worthwhile to paper.

I did not feel tired.

Only a dark numbness.

A melancholy weight of a thousand boulders.

I stared out the window. Watching the light of the sun touch the dew dropped field. I heard a sound behind me. I turned and saw Erwin standing in the doorway.

His eyes were red rimmed, and I could see where he had wiped tear marks from his face. He sniffed and looked at me.

"Come in, Erwin," I said.

He walked over to a chair and sat, looking out the window.

"Have you been up all night?" he asked.

I nodded. "I have."

He nodded once, looking at the rising sun. I could tell something was building, he was willing the strength to say something.

"I have something for you."

"You do?"

Erwin walked over and dropped a pouch in my lap.

"It's charcoal and parchment. So you can write."

"Erwin…" I looked at him and saw him staring at me.

I could not tell him it would not work. He continued to stare, something else was on his mind.

"Wha—"

"Why are you leaving?" He spun and stared me in the eyes, a pleading look on his face.

"Erwin…" I frowned, though I didn't mean to. "What do you mean? We spoke about this yesterday."

He shook his head. "You told me you were called because you were a knight, but why are you leaving?"

"What do you mean?" I scooted my chair closer to my son.

"You could abandon the knights. You could take us and flee. We could keep running across the countryside. Be together forever. Why don't we do that? Why do you have to leave?"

I sighed and looked down.

"You know I cannot do that, Erwin."

"Because of duty? Because of honor?" asked Erwin.

"Partly, but more than that."

"I don't understand." Erwin hung his head. "I know I should not be weak like this, but I don't want you to leave."

"You are not being weak." I reached out and cupped his chin, raising it so I could look into his eyes. "You are a strong boy. Who told you that you were weak?"

He pulled away from my hand and looked down.

"I know you do what is right. I just…" fresh tears sprung to his eyes, "I want you here with me, with mother. As a family."

His bleary eyes locked with mine.

"We're happy…why change that?"

My heart twisted.

"Could it be otherwise…I would change it."

"But it can be." Erwin made a fist and pounded it against the chair's arm. "Flee, run. I know duty and honor matter, but what about us? What about happiness?"

Erwin's eyes lowered.

"What good is duty? What good is honor if they take my father away from me? Surely such a thing cannot be good?"

He looked back up, hoping for an answer I did not know how to give.

"I…"

My voice faltered. I sat back in my chair and looked out at the sunrise, as if it would have the answers.

"I don't know, son."

"But you're still going to go?"

"I…I have to."

I looked at Erwin. He looked down, deep in thought.

"I don't want you to go," he said.

"I know. I don't want to go either."

He looked up at me. "So why go?"

I took a deep breath. Something crystalized for me.

"Because I love you."

"What?" Erwin leaned back, staring at me like I had sprouted a second head. "You're leaving because you love me? I wish you didn't love me then. At least I'd have a father."

Erwin's voice choked at the end of his sentence; tears fell again. I held up my hand.

"I know. I understand how you feel, Erwin…" My voice was raspy, tears threatened to spring from my eyes.

I gulped and cleared my throat. Erwin wiped his face, clearing the tears. He stared at me, expecting an answer.

"Horrors are coming, Erwin. Things you have never seen, never experienced. Horror that would destroy me, destroy you, destroy your mother. Your friends, your home, everyone you know. They'd all be dead."

I leaned forward.

"I'm going to try to stop those horrors from reaching you and your mother. I will do anything I can to make sure what I have seen never happens to you and her. Even if that means leaving, even if that means…dying."

The word was out. Saying it made me feel like I was out of breath. It made me feel like someone had punched me in the gut. My mouth opened and closed a few times. I felt faint. Erwin stared at me, his eyes wide.

He stood up and rushed from the room. I slammed my head into my hands, rubbing vigorously at my eyes. I groaned. That was not how I meant that to come out. I felt a soft hand on my shoulder.

I looked up and saw Josephine looking down at me. Her eyes were wet. She knelt and draped herself over me.

"I know why you go, dear husband," she said.

Her strength helped to keep me afloat.

"And I want you to know these things."

She held me fast.

"I will always love you and only you. And Erwin and I both know…"

Her voice cracked. She paused a moment, then continued.

"That you love us more than anything. So, know this. We love you more than anything. No matter what the future holds, no matter what transpires, no matter what happens."

She shifted, so she was staring me in the eyes.

"I know why you go. You go for honor, you go for duty, but above all you go for love." She leaned forward and placed her forehead against mine.

We closed our eyes.

"I love you, Alaric."

"I love you too."

"I know."

A horn sounded. Cutting through the air like a spearpoint through tender flesh. Our eyes opened. I looked out at the sun now rising over the hill. There was only one horn that would sound all the way out here.

The horn of the city.

The horn of the breach.

The time had come. I stood up. I pulled Josephine close and held her tight. The tears stopped. Something else was taking its place. Something familiar. Something I had experienced first in training and then in battle.

A mix of numbness and coolness.

I looked down at her.

"I'll see you again," I said.

She nodded. "And I you."

I went out to the stable and saddled my horse.

I looked back and saw Josephine and Erwin standing side by side. I walked over and hugged them both.

"Until we meet again," I said.

I said it with a confidence I did not feel.

"Know I love you both." I said, backing away towards my horse. "More than life itself. You two are the only thing worth that."

Erwin looked at me. Tears filled his eyes. He opened his mouth as if wanting to speak but no words came out. I grabbed his shoulder and squeezed.

"Be strong."

Then I mounted and rode.

Chapter 10

It amazes me how fast things change.

I rode to the council chamber, a knight took my horse, then they whisked me far below the chamber into a darkened room. Two guards draped in red robes guarded the entrance to the room. They parted to allow me entrance.

Immediately, I saw Fion and Warin in a corner. Around them were many other unfamiliar faces. I walked towards my two brother knights. A tall man stepped in front of me.

I looked up at him. He wore a grim frown and had a rectangular shaped head. Atop his head he wore a rectangular hat with oranges hues. I took a step back and saw the man's folded robes matched his hat.

A confessor.

"I have no sins to confess, sir," I said. "I am but a simple knight and have no taste for the whip or the iron."

The man frowned.

"Alaric."

I turned and saw Septimus hobble towards me, supporting himself on a cane. He stopped between me and the tall man.

"This is Cornelius, Alaric. A confessor of the highest order."

I gave a slight bow to Cornelius.

"Come to see us off?" I asked.

"You misunderstand," said Septimus. "Cornelius, and everyone else is in this room, except me of course, is going with you."

"What?"

I looked beyond Septimus, trying to study the faces in the candlelit darkness.

"You heard me," replied Septimus.

"Alaric," said Cornelius.

I looked over, locking eyes with the confessor. I immediately felt weighed, judged, and found wanting.

"Yes."

Cornelius extended his hand.

"Pleasure to meet you."

I took his hand and shook it.

"Where is your armor?" asked Cornelius. "We are to set out soon. I would have expected you to be ready."

"What?"

Cornelius frowned. "No matter. We'll begin on time anyway." He nodded towards me. "Nice meeting you, Alaric."

I nodded back. Cornelius paced off with Septimus. I walked over to Fion and Warin. Another man stood by them.

He was the opposite of the confessor. This man wore a leather vest over a frayed shirt. His belly pressed against his shirt. He wore ragged trousers and boots. A pack was slung at his side. In his hand, he held a flask he knocked back to his lips.

"Alaric," said Warin. "Come here."

I walked over. "Warin, what's going on?"

"Council orders," said Alaric. "We're going in as a team."

I glanced around. "Who...who are all these people?"

It was hard to see in the darkness, but I had counted at least a half dozen companions.

"Priests, nobles, and hey, Alaric."

I turned to Warin.

"I want you to meet Hunter."

Warin held out a hand to the man in the leather vest. The man stepped forward into the candlelight of a nearby table. He wore a green cap with a pheasant's feather sticking out of it. He held out a hand.

"Pleasure to meet you, Sir Alaric."

I took the man's hand. "Pleasure is mine, I'm sure."

"Hunter is the man that made all this possible."

"What?" I asked.

"He's been to the other side and back. He's going to lead us through. He has a map and everything. He's going to take us and take us back out."

I snapped back to Hunter, staring at him with a new appreciation. Suddenly the stubbly ill-kept man before me became a legend, a hero.

"You've been?" I asked.

Hunter nodded once. "Sure have." He knocked back more of his flask. "And lived to tell the tale." He winked and gave a little laugh.

I looked at Warin, then back to Hunter.

"I…I didn't know anyone had breached in ages."

Hunter smiled a mischievous smile. "Well, the council doesn't share all it does." He stepped back. "But they're paying me a handsome fee to get you all in there and back as fast as possible," he laughed. "And alive, of course."

"That'd be preferable," I said.

Hunter laughed and smacked my shoulder. Something caught his eye, and he moved deeper into the room, away from us. I looked at Fion.

"What is going on, brother?"

Fion shrugged, tightening a strap on Warin's back. "I'm just as lost as you, friend."

I heard clapping behind me and looked back. The red guards had entered the room and stood on either side of Septimus. The guards held candelabras that lit up the space in front of them.

"Gather around," said Septimus, holding out his hands. "A brief message before we leave and, of course, a prayer. Brother Matthew, would you please come lead us?"

"It would be my honor."

A soft voice spoke from the crowd. A portly monk in a simple monk's habit stepped forward. He had a shaved head and rosy cheeks. He turned towards the group, a brilliant smile beamed across his face.

"Let us pray."

The monk led us in a traditional prayer. We finished and Septimus stepped forward again.

Septimus held up a hand and said, "I know many things have changed and many of you may be confused right now. But know that we spent long hours at the council deliberating this."

Septimus cleared his throat.

"What we have assembled before us is a diverse group with a diverse set of skills. We have nobles, monks, knights, a mystic, and a cartographer. Together, you will be strong. Together you can overcome the darkness that lies in the fallen kingdom."

Septimus' voice rose as he spoke.

"You can overcome together. Together, you can break the cracks. Together, you can save our world."

Septimus looked around the room, looking ten years younger.

"Were I a few years younger, I would journey with you, but alas, this task is not for me. Know this, on the other side things will change. Your need for food and water will whittle to nothing. You will feel neither tired nor awake. You will not need to sleep or drink.

Septimus' eyes roamed the room. They settled on me.

"You are there to slay demons. To weaken the power of their world until the cracks relent. Just as others that have breached before have done. Just like the mighty Aldin."

Septimus threw his hands towards the back of the room. We all turned. The guards had moved and stood with their candelabras raised, highlighting a magnificent marble statue. A statue we knights knew all too well.

Aldin the Unchallenged.

The only man to enter the fallen world alone and seal the cracks by himself. A legendary knight. I glanced around the room. Others looked at the statue with awe. It seems Aldin's legend extended beyond the lore of the knights.

Septimus cleared his throat. We looked back at him.

"In a few hours we you will all journey to the fallen kingdom together, with the great Hunter as your guide. You will rely on him for every step but know...your faith could not be placed in better hands. But before then...we prepared a feast.

They escorted us from the dim chamber into a large dining hall. One long table sat in the middle, filled with choice meats and drink. They seated us at the table. I sat across from the cartographer, Hunter and the monk, Matthew.

Cornelius, the confessor, sat next to Matthew and didn't seem happy about the situation. Further down I saw a hulking brute of a man, a thin man dressed in finery, and an old man with a tall conical wide-brimmed hat on his head, a grey bushy beard hid his face from me.

I looked over at Fion.

"What is this? What have we gotten ourselves into?"

"One hell of a feast," said Hunter, reaching across the table and yanking at a turkey leg.

The monk, Matthew, leaned forward.

"Dear knights." He looked at me, a warmth shined from his eyes. "Forgive me, but I have not had the opportunity to introduce myself."

He extended a pudgy hand across the table.

"My name is Matthew and I am a brother of the Sanatius Brotherhood. It is my sincere pleasure to meet you, Sir Knight."

I grabbed his hand. "Alaric, and the pleasure is mine."

Sanatius. I had heard of them. Monks specialized in the healing arts. An excellent companion to have when venturing into the fallen world.

My heart ached. All the new people had distracted me from what I left behind.

"I know you are giving up much," said Matthew.

His words caught me off guard. I looked up and looked into his eyes.

"Many are, but I see the pain in your eyes. You're walking away from more than most. I want you to know that I will be here to support you through this journey, whatever may come."

"Thank…thank you," I said.

The confessor eyed Matthew like he was a festering sore.

"You're a kind man, Matthew," said Hunter, shoving a hunk of bread into his mouth. "Kinder than me."

"Nonsense," said Matthew. "You're the only one that's been and is going back. You're risking more than anyone here."

Matthew placed a hand on Hunter's back.

"You are the kind one."

Hunter shrugged as he chewed. Matthew turned and saw Cornelius stared at him.

"Something wrong, confessor?" asked Matthew.

Cornelius smiled.

"Many things, my dear friend. Many things."

Matthew shook his head and turned to Alaric. He gestured over his shoulder at Cornelius.

"This one will never find satisfaction."

"No," said Cornelius. "No, I won't. Not until the work of God is complete in this world."

"That's a tiring game, my friend," said Matthew.

"It's no game, my misguided brother and…" Cornelius leaned closer to him. "Someone has to do it."

Matthew shook his head and looked at the food.

"I think we've talked enough. Why don't we eat?"

I did my best to eat. But I had little appetite. My thoughts drifted to the woman and boy I had left at home. Sometime during the meal, I felt a hand on my shoulder. It was Warin.

"Eat, Alaric. You'll need strength for the task ahead."

"I thought Septimus said we would have no need of food in the fallen world."

"You won't when you're there. It's the getting there you'll need food for."

Warin turned and tore into his third slice of beef. I did my best to finish my plate. I glanced around the room. Most of the people seemed to enjoy themselves, even Hunter, who had been there before.

Was I the one missing something?

Or were they?

Chapter 11

We sang hymns after dinner. Then Septimus brought us to a deeper chamber. To the well. We all stood in a circle, all nine of us.

Septimus nodded to each of us as he spoke our names.

Warin, Master Knight of the Order.

Fion, Knight of the Order.

Alaric. Knight of the Order.

Cornelius, Confessor of the High Church.

Hunter, Cartographer.

Matthew, Sanatius Monk.

Septimus' eyes focused on the large, brutish looking man. He was young, his head shaved, his armor polished with gold.

Alexei, House of Grigorov

Septimus' eyes flicked to a man, almost a boy, with a slight built. He wore fine, tailored clothing and had tousled curly hair.

Sacha, House of Grigorov

Brothers, it seems.

Finally, Septimus turned to the wizened old man. The brim of his hat concealed his face. I noticed traces of a silver moon and stars on his hat. His grey robes hid his figure. He held a wooden staff in his gnarled hands.

Ophir, Mystic of the Grand Academy.

Septimus cleared his throat.

"We have all gathered here to answer an ancient call. One that has preserved our humanity through the many trials and tribulations we have been through. We are here to see the completion of an ancient rite. The rite of the blood. The rite of passage."

Septimus drew a knife from his side. He walked over to the well in the center of the circle. I leaned forward and saw it was not a well but a shallow pool of water. Septimus cut into his hand and let the blood flow into the water.

"As Holiness bled for us, so shall we bleed for Thee."

Septimus watched as the blood mingled with the water. He showed no sign of pain, no sign of anything other than devotion to the task.

Septimus looked up.

"You all will go. You will slay the demons that grow and fester in the fallen world. Through their death, you shall weaken the power they hold over our world. Weaken them until the cracks are no more. Then Hunter will see you back to us."

We all glanced at Hunter. He was glassy eyed and smiled. His stubble gave him an eerie look in the faint light.

"Through the ending of life you shall preserve life," said Septimus.

"Bless the blood."

Matthew walked up to Septimus' left side and Cornelius to his right. Matthew proffered a golden urn. Septimus took the urn and removed a stopper from the top. He turned the urn into the well. Red liquid poured from the urn and splashed into the well.

The red liquid spread fast across the water, turning it blood red. Septimus placed the stopper back and handed the urn back to Matthew. Matthew stepped away from the well and returned a moment later, the urn no longer in his possession.

Septimus nodded to Cornelius. Cornelius held out a hand towards the well. He mumbled ancient words, and a faint yellowish light grew from his hands. The light interacted with the blood, flecking it with glowing white spots. Cornelius returned his hand.

Septimus bent over beside the well and rose with a chalice in his hands. He dipped the chalice into the well and turned to Cornelius.

"Drink first, my brother."

Cornelius drank deeply from the cup and passed it to Ophir, who was next to him.

"Drink deeply, my brother," said Cornelius.

We each passed the cup from man to man. Fion passed it to me. I looked into its depths. The cup was still full. I sniffed and the scent of copper filled my nostrils. I set the cup to my lips and drank, closing my eyes.

The liquid was awful, tasting like blood. After I drank, I turned to Warin.

"Drink deep, my brother," I said.

The chalice worked its way back to Septimus. He set it below him, out of sight. I heard stone click onto stone, followed by the trickling of liquid. Septimus stepped back and the well emptied, running through rivulets towards a circular door behind Septimus. One I had not noticed before.

The rivulets filled under the door. There was a shuddering click and then the door gave way, revealing a musty stairway leading down.

"The path is before you," said Septimus. "I hope to see you all again."

Cornelius was the first to enter. I don't know what order we entered after that. I found myself pressed tight against Fion and Warin as he made our way into darkness.

At some point, the door closed behind us and the steps changed. We moved up instead of down. A greenish light shone from above. I looked up and saw the end of the stairs.

Except we walked upstairs and not down them. I paused, Fion bumped into me.

"What is it?" he whispered.

It was the first words I had heard since Septimus and they sounded like the roar of a tiger in the cramped passage. I looked back and turned. Extending my hands in front of me, I felt a solid wall behind us, a wall that had not been there a few moments before. I leaned my head forward and placed it against the wall.

So we were here.

I heard a gasp behind me. I whirled and saw Alexei and Sacha had emerged into the world above. I walked after them. As Matthew and Ophir left the cramped staircase and saw the world beyond, I could hear more gasps.

Warin and Fion blocked me from advancing. They walked as if weighed down by twice the armor they wore.

My armor felt lighter as we walked up the stairs. The green light turned into a green sky with clouds that had a sickly look to them. We walked out of the staircase and into an impossible land.

We were on the ruins of an ancient walkway. Drop offs of leagues on either side. In the distance, across the walkways, I saw the remains of a magnificent castle with crenellated walls and spired towers. I heard myself gasp.

Behind us was a tall mountain range. The peaks tore into the clouds above, the base lost somewhere in the fog of the drops below. I took a step back and hit something solid. I looked down and saw I had hit a stone block, broken from the wall near me.

Then I heard a shout of panic.

I spun. I saw Sacha, the younger of the Grigorov's. He had a hand clasped to a rapier by his side. His eyes were wide, and he stared at something behind a small pile of rubble. Ophir quickly closed the distance to him and pushed the boy aside, staring beyond the rubble.

He froze and took a few steps back, shaking his head.

I glanced at Fion. He raised an eyebrow. We advanced on the rubble together. We walked around and what I saw sent a jolt through my stomach and heart.

It was a man, or what had once been a man. The poor sod's face appeared twisted, and the rest of his body fared little better.

Flesh hung off him. His eyes stared up at the sky. I could see chinbone through a gap in his skin. But there was no smell of decay, no smell of death.

"Things work different here," said Hunter. "While death can be around every corner, decay is not."

I looked over at Hunter. I expected confidence from him, a man who had volunteered to return to such a place. Instead, all I saw was stark fear and doubt on the man's face. I looked back at the twisted body.

"There's more." Alexei spoke from ahead of us.

He had walked up a small set of stairs to a longer walkway. This one piled with carts and rubble. I walked up the stairs and noticed shapes in the corners.

I walked over and saw another man, also dead. His neck twisted, dried blood stained the cobbles below him. Flesh still hung off him in ribbons. As we walked, we discovered more and more of the dead. Though some seemed like they could leap right up and shake your hand.

I moved towards the front of the pack. I had not noticed it until I looked up. There, tied to a stake, was the burnt remains of a priest. His skull hung forward, his robe black tatters. He wore a circlet around his eyes, one that had fused with his bone. A spike ran up his middle and out his back, suspending his corpse above the ground. I heard a whimper escape Matthew behind me.

"Fear not, dear Matthew," said Cornelius, his voice a sneer. "We will prevail."

Behind the priest was another drop off. Ophir looked over the drop off and gasped.

"By all the gods and devils," he whispered.

All of us sped to the edge of the pathway and looked over a small wall to the depths beyond. There lay something beyond understanding. I blinked a few times, tried to understand what it was I looked at.

My mind refused it.

I tried focusing, but my mind refused to make sense of it again. Then it all pieced itself together and my heart slammed in my chest.

A creature lay at the bottom of the ravine. A creature of impossible shape. It had several limbs all jutting this way and that. The creature's limbs had armor covering them and spikes at the ends. The creature's head resembled a man with an elongated snout, snarling teeth jutting out.

The human eyes stared up at us. A spiny tail stuck up behind the creature. Another human face was inside the creature's stomach. One with its eyes pinched and its mouth set in a frown.

I took a step back, feeling sick. Upon hearing Sacha vomit, it was my turn next. I fell to my knees as others heaved.

I heard Matthew sayings 'Oh God' over and over. I looked up and saw Cornelius with one arm folded across his stomach, the other scratched at his chin.

"What have we done?" said Sacha. "What are we dealing with?"

"Peace, brethren," said Warin.

His voice was like a balm to a day old burn.

"Peace."

Warin looked around at the men, a hand on his sword.

"We expected demons when we came here, and demons we have found."

"They're horrible," said Sacha.

Warin nodded. "Indeed, they are."

"What have we done?" asked Hunter.

I looked over and saw the cartographer's eyes were wide. His hand shook as he brought a flask to his lips. He took a swig and shook his head.

My thoughts echoed his words. What had we done? And was there a way back? The panicky fear of never seeing my family again ate at my stomach, nibbled away moment by moment.

I knew it would not be long before there was nothing left of me.

Nothing left of us.

Chapter 12

Hunter, the cartographer, stood ahead of us. He looked over a scarred rocky landscape below. Billowing fog blew high above us, replacing what would be clouds in a normal world. The greenish sheen hung over the land from the fog.

I was neither tired nor awake, neither hungry nor thirsty, neither energized nor weak. It was like my body had entered a state of limbo, like we existed only as ghosts. As spirits wandering this mad land.

Fion was close by my side. He frowned and stared at the cartographer. The cartographer's eyes were glassy. He seemed to be lost.

"I do not trust this fool," said Fion. "Who vetted these people here? Septimus? It's not his skin on the line."

"Peace," I said, more to quell my rising fear than my brother knight's.

"Peace…there is no peace here, Alaric."

"We will make it through, brother."

Fion looked at me, our eyes locked.

"Had anyone else said that, I would not believe them," he smiled. "I am fool enough to believe you."

"Well, keep the foolishness up. It is not yet time to lose hope."

Ophir walked forward, using his staff to navigate the broken cobbles. He walked up a small set of stairs and stood next to Hunter, studying the land below.

"I sense something," said the mystic.

Hunter glanced at the mystic, his eyes widened for a moment before returning to the landscape.

"Hunter." Warin called from the rear. "What do you see? What is the way forward?"

Warin, ever the guardian, had volunteered to be the rear guard. It made me nervous. During our travels I glanced back to check that our mentor and the man I trusted most was still with us, that some phantom had not plucked him from the fog.

Hunter turned to address the group.

"Things…are different, from last I was here but." He held up his hands, offered a weak smile. "It's coming back to me. I know…"

A squawk sounded in the distance. We all turned and saw a raven descend from the sky. It landed on a battlement close to us. It looked down at us, turning its head from side to side.

"A raven?" asked Alexei, moving his bulk as close as he could to the creature. He looked over at Ophir. "Mystic," he said. "What does this portend?"

Ophir studied the raven and shook his head.

"It's but a bird, nobleman."

Alexei looked up at the bird and smiled. He turned to us.

"I cannot say why, but it is nice to see an animal in this wretched land. A boon of home."

Alexei held out his hand towards the raven.

"Little bird, friend. Will you come and rest on my finger?"

The bird squawked and flew off.

"You frighten him," said Sacha, Alexei's brother.

Alexei frowned.

"I would be kind to the bird. He knows that."

Alexei laughed.

It was good to hear his laugh. This bear of a man, at ease in this place. It helped put my own worries to rest. Fion seemed less impressed. He narrowed his eyes.

"Peace, Fion," I said.

Fion looked at me. "What?"

"A laugh is a good thing, right?"

Fion frowned, then nodded. "I guess so."

"Something comes."

Cornelius stood next to Hunter and pointed down the path. We all followed his bony finger to a shambling group of creatures further down. I did a quick count and counted twelve of them.

They looked almost human, though they seemed to be in a state of decay. They drug swords and axes behind them from arms that hung limp. Some wore wooden masks while others had dented helms. They wore rags across their decrepit bodies.

"Demons," said Cornelius, the word like poison to his lips. "We shall kill them all."

Cornelius loosened his mace from his belt and brought it up. He looked back at us. There was a fire burning in his eyes that was fearful.

"Come. Our duty calls us."

Cornelius led us forward. The sounds of scraping metal echoed out; we all readied our weapons. A blue light glowed atop Ophir's staff. I glanced around. Alexei held a hand and a half sword. His brother, Sacha, held a wand in one hand and his rapier in the other.

I looked ahead. The shambling corpses spotted us and headed our way. My heart thudded in my chest. These demons were different from the ones I remember from so long ago. The ones that upended my young life.

They were far less imposing, but still, they filled me with fear. Cornelius led us, as if desperate for battle with the demons. I felt a hand grab my arm. I looked over and stared into Matthew's wide face.

"Have faith, brother," said the monk, a smile creased his cheeks. "We will prevail."

"Thank you," I said.

I turned back to the demons. Ahead of us was a rectangular space, a small set of stairs on either side. We went to meet in the middle of it. We descended the stairs as the demons did on the other side.

I looked at our enemy. I saw black sockets where there should be eyes, their jaws hung loose. These demons were likely men at one point but lost themselves in this place. To the darkness.

I heard a sound like shattering glass and a blue ball rush forward and slammed into the first shambler. It tore through him and knocked him off his feet. A moment later there was a sound like a high crystal note and a slim blur of blue energy slashed into another's throat. The creature toppled forward.

And then we met.

I rushed forward to engage with a creature dragging an ax behind it. It went to bring the ax around, but my sword was already moving. My blade pierced through its rags and into where the heart would be if it was still human.

The creature crumpled against the cobbles. I withdrew my sword, a black ichor along the blade, and turned. I felt, rather than saw, the blow coming for me. I twisted as another creature's club smacked against my pauldron and crashed into my face.

The force of the blow dispersed, but it was a still a club to face. I twisted with the blow, breaking some of the strength, but my jaw still ached. If it hadn't been set, I would have had missing teeth.

As I spun around, I witnessed Fion rush forward and decapitate my aggressor. I took a step back and grabbed my jaw. I winced. Fion nodded to me. I glanced around. The battle was over. But we were far from unharmed.

Sacha had a gash across his face. He touched his face and pulled away his hand. He stared at the blood as if it was something he had never seen before. Alexei crashed next to him. The brute was unharmed and grabbed Sacha.

"Are you okay, brother?" he asked.

I looked over and saw Warin help Ophir to his feet. Cornelius turned around, the creature at his feet a smoking husk. A white light faded from the end of his mace. I observed Fion had one eye shut and blackened.

He shook his head.

"The creature moved so slow, it threw me off."

I nodded. I expected the reactions of a human. All my battles had been learning the timing of a human. These strange creatures threw that. And I had underestimated them. Judging by all the bumps and bruises, we had all underestimated them.

Blood soaked Hunter's torn shirt. He patted at it with a handkerchief he produced from his vest. He held a clean ax in his hand.

Warin walked towards me, helping Matthew along. The monk had a band tied around his head, the band was soaked with blood. I shook my head.

These creatures were nothing compared to what was legend to be in this land. I looked up at the sky and saw the cracks there. Large, ghastly, and unmoved by our slaying.

Warin looked up, then at me. Our eyes met, and we shared an understanding.

We did not know what we had gotten ourselves into.

Chapter 13

The hopelessness soon turned to anger in my gut. We crested a small hill made of rubble, a tall wall on either side of us. Hunter led the way. We had established we needed to find shelter after that last battle, a place to recuperate and rest.

Hunter said he knew of such a place and that it was just over the hill of rubble we traversed. Behind lay the remnants of a long dead village. Hunter crested the top of the hill and shielded his eyes, studying the landscape beyond.

Hunter had seemed distant and melancholy since we had entered the land. A smile spread across his face for the first time. He spun to us and pointed behind.

"I've found it. Its here."

Shelter.

Fion rushed forward with Sacha. They crested the hill and followed Hunter's finger. Fion turned away like lightning had struck him and shook his head. Sacha stared at it, speaking after a few moments.

"It just a bunch of lumpy rocks," said Sacha.

"Rocks that will provide cover and rest," replied Hunter, smacking Sacha on the back.

Sacha frowned and stared at Hunter. Hunter looked down.

"Sorry."

I walked up next to the two and looked out. Down from us was another decrepit village, and above that were the remains of a crumpled tower. The first two stories of the tower stood, the second story open to the air above.

"It's not much, but it'll have to do," said Hunter.

"It will do well, friend," said Matthew, patting Hunter on the shoulder as he passed.

We wandered to the structure and went in the front door. Ophir lit up his staff, casting blue light around the room. Light came down from a spiral staircase that went up around the corner to the level overhead.

Ophir found a stool and slumped in the middle of the room. He leaned forward, his staff across his legs. The others found rickety chairs to slump in and walls to slump against. I walked with Fion to the stairs. We glanced up.

Overhead, we could see the green sky. It made me sick if I looked at it for too long. I went and sat along the wall, studying my companions. Matthew sat next to Sacha and murmured something in his ear. Sacha smiled and ate up whatever it was.

Cornelius and Warin sat to my right. Cornelius narrowed his eyes as if expressing disappointment, while Warin closed his eyes. He almost looked asleep.

Warin's eyes flashed open; he glanced around the room.

"A tired lot are we," said Warin.

"Is that a question?" asked Cornelius.

Warin shook his head. "A statement."

"We need to press on soon," Alexei spoke. He had not sat but paced around the room. "Find the biggest one of these things we can and slay it. That has the greatest chance of closing the cracks." He looked over at Ophir. "Is that right, mystic?"

Ophir's eyes were closed, and he didn't seem to notice Alexei had spoken.

"Seems a poor time for meditation, mystic," said Cornelius.

"Friend," said Ophir, his eyes still closed, "This is the best time."

Matthew patted Sacha's knee.

"We need our rest. No point in heading out battered and bruised with no plan."

"Why don't we ask the person who has been here before?" I said.

A few heads turned my way. I waved my hand towards Hunter.

"Hunter," I said, "Where do you think we should go next? Where is the best place from which to slay demons and bring this quest to its end?"

Hunter looked at me for a few moments, as if unsure of what to say. The entire room looked at him. Hunter shrugged.

"The land has changed. We...demons roam wherever they will. We just have to...go..." Hunter looked at the ground.

I felt bad for him.

"What use was bringing you then?" asked Cornelius.

"Do not be so harsh with him," said Matthew.

Cornelius shook his head. "There is a right way to go about doing this. An effective way." Cornelius pushed himself off the wall and looked around.

"You all saw how even a minor battle can go bad. How we could have easily lost a member of our party or two? You think the danger is much greater going after a large one when we come across it, but I assure you it is not."

Cornelius turned, and I felt his gaze land on me.

"And if we fell one of the big ones, we have a chance to break the cracks. Whereas we could spend our whole time fighting peons and have nothing to show for it. We are trying to take power from this world and, therefore, we must fight the powerful."

Cornelius went back to the wall and rested against it; his arms crossed across his chest.

"That sounds wise to me," said Alexei. "Find the big ones and kill them."

"Do not be so hasty to rush in," Fion said. "Some of you have little experience with battle, but we knights do. If these creatures are as large as the legends say, then they could easily kill us with a sweep of a blade or claw."

Fion looked around the room. "We can ambush the small ones. Set up traps. Whittle them down little by little. Stealing power from this world drip by drip until the cracks close."

"In a year's time?" asked Cornelius. "Others have succeeded. Others have come back and shared their successes with the council who have shared the lessons learned with the High Church. I do not speak from speculation, Sir Knight. I speak from the experience of survivors."

Cornelius smiled. "It is simply the best way."

Fion frowned and leaned back.

"We shall see, I guess."

Warin held up a hand. "Many here make good points. But we still need to decide on a course of action. A goal we can all organize around."

"Slay the strong," said Alexei. "Face them in battle and overcome."

Cornelius nodded along as Alexei spoke. Those were two I did not expect to be on the same page often.

Other voices battered ideas back-and-forth, but they tired me. I stared towards the stairs leading up.

The more they talked, the less hope I felt. It surprised me we hadn't received more direction. The council had briefed Cornelius somewhat, but they had left the rest of us in the dark. What hope was there when we could not even agree where to devote our resources?

I glanced around. Everyone was silent. Had there been a fight? Or was the same realization dawning on everyone?

Frustration grew in my gut. Now was not the time for deliberation, now was the time for action. I stood up, suddenly feeling hemmed in by the walls. I went up the stairs and stood on the ruined second story.

The land stretched out before me. Most of it was the rubble of a former grand kingdom. Far ahead, a chunk of it blocked by the mist, was a gargantuan wall. To the right I saw a church that looked out over a mist filled swamp.

To my left was a great chasm that dropped off leagues below. I bit my lip. It sounded like Cornelius was right. We should go after the most powerful within reason and slay them, though I knew that fighting them in this way only strengthens them.

We cannot solve this with violence.

But what we needed, I wasn't sure, although I knew we would not find it here. Not debating, not tossing ideas to and fro, that meant nothing. We had to venture forth and venture forth now.

I walked back down the stairs.

"I'm going to scout around. To find a way forward, whoever wants to come with me do so. But I will be going."

I walked towards the door leading out. I half-expected someone to stop me, but instead I heard two pairs of boots behind me.

I turned and saw Fion and Hunter.

"Let's go," I said.

Chapter 14

Hunter stood outside, his face set and grim. We looked across a world of grey rubble. Shattered cobbles stretched as far as we could see, ruined buildings dotted the path. Steep drop offs on either side gave us one way forward.

Ahead was a great wall shrouded by the green tinged fog. Hunter scratched his chin. He looked back at me. Fion and I stared at him. He bit his lip, then turned back to the wall.

"Well?" asked Fion.

"Hold...hold on," said Hunter, holding up a hand.

"You recognize anything?" asked Fion.

"I..." Hunter scanned the horizon.

His eyes darted around, as if desperate for something familiar, something to cling to. His hand reached inside his vest then he yanked it back out.

His eyes focused on something. He clapped his hands, then pointed.

"There. There, I see something familiar."

I glanced at Fion. The look of mistrust was clear. He looked over at me. Our eyes met.

He didn't trust Hunter, and neither did I.

"Come on." Hunter started forward, navigating down a rubble strewn slope.

We followed him through the wreckage. As we went, I saw more bodies, some of men that had ventured here in years past and others of misshapen creatures that should only exist in nightmares.

One stood out to me. At first glance, it looked like a child, small limbs and a bloated belly. But a beak emerged from the mouth and the eyes, though partly closed, were red and pupilless. A blade had been attached to the end of the creature's hands as if by some mad seamstress.

I shuddered as we walked by, one hand gripped tight to my sword, less the thing come alive.

Hunter moved down the path. He climbed up an overlook and nodded to a well at the top.

"I remember this well." His voice was shaky, but he seemed to tell the truth.

"Does that aid us?" asked Fion. "I thought you knew the best way through this land."

Hunter stared at the well, ignoring Fion's glare.

Hunter licked his lips and walked to the well. He set his hands on the side and investigated its depths. His eyes misted for a moment.

"I remember this place." He whispered again.

"So, what is the path forward?" I asked. "The quickest way to the demons that we need to slay."

Hunter chuckled, it set me on edge. He shook his head, still staring into the depths of the well.

"What are we doing here…madness, madness to the last."

"Hunter." I walked forward and set a hand on the cartographer's shoulder.

"Hunter," I repeated.

He glanced over his shoulder at me. There was an eerie light in his eyes that had not been there before.

"Are you alright?" I asked.

Hunter nodded. "As alright as one can be in this place."

He looked across the landscape. At the broken cobbles, the ruined homes, and the cliffs that fell off to either side, dipping into nothingness.

"What a wasteful land," he said.

Hunter looked down the path and shook his head.

"It keeps changing. A map. I can't make a map of this place. How can you make a map of moving water? A map of melting snow? It's madness. This is madness."

His voice rose and his eyes widened.

"Hunter," I said, trying to keep my voice firm.

"Do you recognize nothing? Nothing at all?"

He chuckled again. That unnerving chuckle of a man threatening to go mad.

"Why did I come back? What did I think?" He smacked a hand against his head. "So foolish."

"Hunter," Fion spoke. "Get it together."

Hunter smiled, it was unnerving.

"What is there to get together, knight?" He held up his hands towards the land beyond. "Last time there was the rubble, but it was…different. And that great wall beyond, I have never seen that before."

He looked around.

"These cliffs. There was not a cliff before, but an ocean. Where is the ocean now?"

"You don't recognize any of this?" I grabbed Hunter's shoulders and twisted him so he could face me. "Nothing?"

Hunter looked up at the sky.

"There are…similarities. Here and there. The rubble, the sky."

I released his shoulders. "Perhaps you were in another part then?"

"No…the entrance was the same."

"And it took you so long to say this why?" asked Fion. "You've led us on all this time without letting us know?" Fion walked forward as if to strike Hunter.

I halted him an arm's length away.

"We are all on the same side here," I said.

"Are we?" asked Fion, glaring at Hunter. "If so, then he would have said something."

Hunter held up a shaking hand.

"Can you get us back home?" I asked, a growing fear gnawed at my stomach.

"I…" Hunter nodded. "We will find the way."

A bit of his old self seemed to return. He smiled.

"Some things are familiar. I know the way back."

"It closed behind us," said Fion. "Did that happen last time?"

Hunter nodded. "It will remain closed. Until the cracks are no longer in the sky." Hunter gestured up to the cracks. "The way opens back up after that."

"There have not been cracks in years. How are you sure?" I asked.

"The council." Hunter nodded up and down in an exaggerated motion. "Most certainly. We'll be back. There…" He chuckled and shook his head. "There are things coming back to me now."

He looked at Fion. "Sorry, the land overwhelmed me for a moment. But there are paths I am remembering. Things shifted, but not as much as I thought. We go forward to the great wall and beyond that we'll find the larger demons. The ones we can bring down to close the cracks."

He laughed and stretched out his hand, grabbing my shoulder.

"Thanks for helping me. Getting me out of my mood. I was just taken for a loop, but I think everything is fine now. Surely the land has set you off your normal base, no? Not even a little?"

Of course the land had. It had to all of us. But I still didn't trust Hunter.

I glanced at Fion. His eyes showed hostility, he turned from Hunter.

"That great wall in the distance there? That's where we go?" asked Fion.

Hunter nodded. "Yes, that's it. Beyond there is the fallen world proper, so to speak. There are many places there. Great cities, ancient forests. But we'll find what we're looking for, what we need there. Yes, I know that for certain."

I stared at the wall in the distance. It seemed so far away. But without sleep, without stopping for breaks, eating, or drinking, distances were not the same as they were back in our world.

"Alright," I said. "Then we return to the others, and we find a way forward. We—"

Something massive moved in the distance. Something impossible. About halfway between the wall and where we stood, a great shape climbed out of the drop off.

It had great spindly legs like an insect's. The green light from above reflected off the armor covering its body. It had a long stalk neck, at the end of which sprouted three veiled heads. The creature towered over the buildings it walked between.

Fear gripped me, right behind it, madness. What I looked at was impossible. Both its size and its existence. The creature walked across the path and down the other side of the drop off.

The creature was gone for a full minute before I realized we had not moved. I closed my gaping mouth and looked at the others. I saw the same emotions there that swirled inside me.

Fear.

And hopelessness.

Chapter 15

We walked across the broken landscape towards the great wall in the distance. We occasionally heard groans sound up from the drop off on either side, but we had not seen any other creatures.

Ophir stared at Hunter as we walked.

"So tell me again," said Ophir. "It was beyond the walls that you saw the great tree?"

Hunter looked like he wanted to crawl into a hole and die.

"Yes," said Hunter. "That's where I saw it."

Ophir picked at his beard, mulling over Hunter's words.

"And there were four castles there?" asked Ophir.

Hunter scratched at his neck.

"So much happened."

"Is that not what you said?" pressed Ophir.

Hunter looked around as if there was a way to escape from the questioning.

"Answer him," said Fion, standing on the other side of me.

"Let him think, Fion," said Warin.

Fion turned to Warin and nodded. He looked back at Hunter, expecting an answer.

"Yes...of course." Hunter managed an uneasy smile. "That's what I said. These questions." Hunter waved a hand as if shooing us off. "They are too much. I will guide you. Trust me on that."

Hunter glanced around at the group.

"Look, we have powerful knights, noblemen, mystics, priests, and more. We will be fine."

Hunter's smile threatened to split the side of his face again.

"Give me time to think I will lead us right."

I glanced back at Warin. He frowned but said nothing.

"But...the tree," said Ophir. "It is beyond the walls?"

"Yes," said Hunter, staring ahead. "Beyond the wall."

"Statues," said Ophir. "Were there statues there?"

"What?" Hunter glanced at the mystic, then back to the path. "Yes, many a statue."

"Dragons. Did you see statues of dragons?" asked Ophir.

"Dragons?" Hunter cocked his head to the side. "Sure, there were dragons. Plenty of them."

"Plenty of them?" Ophir's voice held excitement.

I looked over at the mystic. There was a spark of something glittering in his eye. It felt strange.

"Sure, great colossal statues. Some life sized or at least, what I'd imagine life sized dragons to be."

Ophir looked down, his eyes snapped back and forth like he read an invisible book. A smile came to his lips, and he stepped back, letting Hunter take the lead. I looked up. We were close to the wall.

The wall rose from the depths of the drop off and went up, clouds touched the battlements high above. Our path led towards a great opening in the wall.

"Do you recognize this path, Hunter?" asked Warin.

"Of course," said Hunter.

The cartographer slipped the flask from his side and took a drink. He sighed and tucked it away.

"You're going heavy on your medicine, are you not?" asked Fion.

Hunter smiled. "Friend, one can never go too heavy with medicine. I know what you think." He turned to Fion. "But you'd be wrong."

I looked back at the looming wall. We were getting close. There was no way to tell the passage of time here. No matter what, I never felt tired, nor hungry, or thirsty. The light never changed and counting time was madness.

As we neared the wall a crest of land rose ahead of us, blocking the view of the wall's entrance. I could only make out the top of the gap where light shone through.

I thought back to that strange creature we had seen crawl out of the drop off. The thought sent a shiver down my spine. I jogged ahead, ascending the crest and expected to see safe passage.

Instead, I saw a yawning gap a stone's throw across. The path led between the wall on the other side. My heart skipped a beat. I whirled and locked eyes with Hunter.

His eyes widened.

"Hunter."

I stomped towards him. He turned as if to run. Fion grabbed him and whirled him around to face me.

I pointed to the rise behind me.

"What is this?"

"What is what?" asked Hunter.

I grabbed his vest and yanked him up the rise. We stood, overlooking the substantial drop off below.

"Where is the path?"

"Oh…" Hunter grabbed his at chest. "This…this is different."

I pushed him back down the rise.

"You don't know the way forward." The others gathered behind Hunter, forming a semi-circle around him. Hunter glanced around like a trapped animal.

"Hold." Warin stepped out from the group, held his hands out.

"Hunter," said Warin.

Hunter looked at Warin.

"You said things have changed."

Hunter nodded.

"Now be truthful with us. This path…had you ever been on it?"

"Sure, I—"

Warin's dark gaze silenced the cartographer. He glanced around, looked like he was about to cry. The cartographer hung his head and walked to the edge of the gap. He looked down.

"Hunter," said Warin. "We need an answer, friend."

Hunter spun, the force of his spin made me step back, a hand grasped to my sword. His eyes widened and there was anger there. He yanked his ax from his side and glared at all of us.

"Back, back, you pack of dogs."

Hunter swiped through the air in front of him. I glanced at Warin. He stared at Hunter with his arms crossed, looking more like a disappointed father than anything else. I went to draw my sword.

"Peace," said Warin.

I released my sword.

Hunter looked over at me.

"This…this damn land." Tears sprung to his eyes.

He looked back at the group.

"I didn't know what this was. They told me I'd get gold if I explored. They told all of us that and we, they, they're all dead. Every one of them, except me. And we didn't…" Hunter shook his head. "We didn't explore this land. There is no exploring this land. There is only death…"

Hunter shook his head.

"I didn't want to come here. They didn't give me a choice."

Cornelius stepped to the front of the group, stood level with Warin.

"Who did not give you a choice?" asked Cornelius, his permanent frown on his face.

"I had debt to pay. I thought this would be better than that, but I was wrong. They asked if I knew the way. I have debt to pay so I said yes. We need to turn back. We need to get back."

"How did you get back last time?" asked Warin.

"I…I don't know."

More tears streaked down Hunter's face.

"I don't know. They were all dead. Billy, my brother. He carried me. They took him. I survived. I don't know, but I woke back there. I know nothing. I told them I did. I needed the money. But I shouldn't have. This place, nothing is worse than this place."

"So, you've led us all to our dooms," said Cornelius. "All so a drunkard could pay off his debts."

Hunter took a step back. His boot slipped off the edge, sending pebbles down into the depths.

"I…I didn't think. I, I don't know."

"You've killed us," said Fion.

"We are not dead yet, Fion." said Warin, his voice like iron.

Fion stepped back and looked down.

"Hunter." said Warin. "You don't know the way forward."

Hunter shook his head. "I know nothing, only that this land contains horrors beyond your wildest imaginations."

Hunter glanced back at the abyss. What he was about to do was written on his face. Hunter went to leap. I tackled him midair and brought him to the ground. We rolled down the slope. Many hands reached for Hunter, yanking him from my grasp.

I saw knives out. Warin leapt in among them, driving the crowd back. I stood up, rushing to Warin's side.

I saw hostile faces.

"Kill him," said the confessor. "It's more than he deserves."

"We will not kill him," said Warin. "That accomplishes nothing."

"He must pay for his crimes."

"Then he will do so by serving the group."

Sides were being drawn. Some drifted off towards Warin while others drifted towards the confessor.

We were being divided.

Chapter 16

"You cannot allow him to escape justice, knight," said Cornelius, staring at Warin.

"And he will not," replied Warin, meeting Cornelius' gaze.

Alexei walked up behind Cornelius and looked down at Hunter.

"Dishonorable," said Alexei as if speaking to himself.

He shook his head.

"We should execute him by the sword, and even that may be too lenient."

I looked at Hunter. He shivered and curled up on himself. His ax lay at his side. His eyes darted around and snot dribbled from his nose. He looked like a child before the gallows. I sighed and shook my head.

I walked forward, standing next to Warin.

"Slaying him won't do anything. He's another man with an ax. One that has been here before, even if it was not in the same capacity that he told us."

Sweat trickled down my neck. The hostile eyes looked at me. Things could go bad, terrible.

Ophir walked next to Cornelius, shaking his head.

"Was what you said about the dragons true?" asked Ophir.

Cornelius whirled on Ophir, raising an eyebrow.

"Is that what you are concerned with, mystic?"

Ophir ignored Cornelius, staring at Hunter.

"Was it true?" pressed Ophir.

"Hold now." Matthew walked out from behind the crowd and knelt by Hunter, placing a hand on his shoulder.

Cornelius rolled his eyes and glanced away.

"We cannot hope to save our world by taking the life of Hunter. He made a mistake, yes. As we all have—"

"I have never led eight men to their deaths," said Cornelius.

"And neither has Hunter," replied Matthew. "We still live and we would have come on this journey anyways."

Alexei held a hand out towards Hunter.

"But he was supposed to be our guide. He failed in this and now we are without a guide."

"The same would happen if he were to be struck down," said Warin. "By a monster or our own hand. We would still be down a guide."

"But he is not our guide." Cornelius pointed a bony finger at Hunter. "He is a liar, a deceiver, and a drunkard."

Matthew glared at Cornelius. "None of which makes him worthy of death."

Cornelius breathed in, his face turned red. "You soft-hearted fool. Just like your witless founder. Why the council brought a broken-hearted sore from the Sanatius Brotherhood I shall never know."

Matthew stood up and stomped towards Cornelius, a pudgy finger pointed.

"Now look here, you pompous, heartless ass."

"Men…" said Warin, a warning tone in his voice. "Let's not get personal here."

Matthew stopped a step from Cornelius. The two looked like they were about to come to blows.

"What the High Church never understood in their golden palaces and with their books of wisdom is that God is love." A passion beamed from Matthew's eyes. "God is love, above all else."

Cornelius swatted Matthew's finger aside. "God is order, you bloated fool. Now step aside so we can mete out justice."

"Hold." Warin stepped between Hunter and Cornelius. "Brother Confessor, please," said Warin.

Cornelius looked at Warin, studying him. He went to say something, then closed his mouth. His eyes roamed behind Warin and settled on Fion.

"Brother Knight," said Cornelius.

Fion looked up.

"Do you not agree that this wretch deserves death?"

Fion looked at Hunter. Hunter looked up at Fion. Fion sighed.

"Yes…but I'll follow my commander and whatever he says."

Cornelius sighed, the man seemed to visibly deflate.

"Very well."

He pulled himself back up to his full height.

"We need to continue this journey. We—"

"I…" Hunter's voice was so weak I was not entirely sure he had spoken.

We all looked down at the wretched man.

"I know a way."

Cornelius shook his head, placing his hands to his temples.

"Hunter…if you think any will believe you."

"Let him speak," said Matthew.

"Well, except that one, of course." Cornelius rolled his eyes and walked a few paces off, as if done with the whole situation.

"I know of another way. I remember it," said Hunter. "When we fled. It's a way to the interior. A way to the larger demons. The ones that if we kill…we can change things."

"You know a way in?" asked Warin.

Cornelius made a sound of disapproval. He waved Ophir over and they walked out of earshot. I looked at Hunter. The man sniffed and wiped at his nose.

"I know a way. I'm sure of it this time. When we were running, I saw it. A way in."

Hunter cleared his throat and looked around. He locked on Matthew, the only friendly face in the crowd.

"Alexei," called Ophir.

Alexei walked over to the separate group.

"This place. I think there's a pattern to it. It's…can you help me up?" asked Hunter.

Matthew snaked out a hand and grabbed Hunter, yanking him up. Hunter got to his feet and dusted himself off.

"I…I didn't see it before, but I mean it this time." Hunter looked at Warin.

"Trust me. I can get us in there. We didn't quite make it that far last time, but we were right on the cusp. If we had a little more time before that thing came…we would have made it."

Warin scratched his chin. He looked at me. I shrugged. He looked back at Hunter.

"What is this way in?"

"Gentlemen." Cornelius walked back to the circle.

We all looked at him.

"Ophir thinks he knows the way forward."

Ophir looked at us.

"There is an energy in this land. One that those attuned can sense. And I believe it leads the way deeper in. To the great demons that we must slay."

They were all looking at Warin. who looked like he'd rather be anywhere else in the world. Warin looked at Hunter.

"We'll have to agree on a path. We cannot split up."

"If you're trusting him," said Cornelius, nodding to Hunter. "Then there is not a man among us who would follow you."

"I'll follow," said Fion.

"As will I."

The words slipped out, more reflex than anything else. Cornelius nodded.

"Then I will respect your decisions. However, I will follow Ophir as will Alexei and…" Cornelius turned and found Sacha.

"What of you Sacha?"

Sacha crossed his arms. He shook, his eyes darting left and right. He looked up.

"I will go where Alexei goes."

Cornelius nodded and turned back to Warin.

"You shall have your knights and the doddering fool. At least your knights should be of some use."

Matthew glared but said nothing.

"And of course, you'll have the so-called cartographer."

Cornelius frowned. "We shall go our own way and wish you the best on yours."

"No." Warin made a chopping motion with his hand. "We cannot split up. Not here."

"Then we shall all follow Ophir."

"Let Hunter speak," said Warin. "Say what he knows of the way forward."

"Perhaps we need some time to decide," said Matthew. "Let us cool off for a bit. That may be what is best for everyone."

Cornelius folded his arms within his robes.

"Time is of the essence."

"We know," said Warin. "Let us discuss this and we will figure out the best way forward."

The two groups diverged. We went over to the remnants of a long-destroyed building while the others went and sat by the drop off. I was not sure what we had to discuss or what the separation would yield.

But I knew it made me uneasy. This was not a safe land.

Here, separation could quickly lead to death.

Chapter 17

I wiped a hand across my face. Warin stood in front of me, Fion to the right. The two of them talked for what felt like hours. I saw Cornelius and Ophir off to the right, talking in hushed voices.

Alexei and Sacha stood over Hunter, staring at him. Matthew sat behind Hunter, as if guarding him. I scratched my neck. I was getting restless. The less time we were in this land, the better.

I thought of Septimus' words, turned them over in my head. He wanted us to kill the demons, slay enough, and the cracks would break. Then we could return home. The idea didn't sit right with me. Violence begets more violence, not peace.

Agitating the demons of this land would only lead to destruction, but I didn't know enough about the land to find another way forward. I looked at Ophir. He nodded to something Cornelius said.

I wondered what he knew that we didn't. The man had deep knowledge about many things, the land around us being one of them. But I could be wrong. It might just be his robe, beard, and hat that made me think he was a possessor of esoteric knowledge.

I glanced around at the companions. We were still too far apart from each other for my comfort. Something Fion, the constant worrier that he was, had pointed out multiple times.

"They will come around," said Warin.

Fion shook his head.

"I don't think they will, Warin. You always think the best of people but…" Fion glanced around. "We're dividing further by the minute."

"I will not allow that to happen," snapped Warin.

We both stared at Warin for a moment. It was so unlike him to snap. He looked down for a moment as if ashamed.

"Sorry, Fion…"

Fion held up a hand. "My apologies. You are wiser than me."

Warin shook his head. "I am far from wise."

He looked up and took a deep breath. "We need unity. To find a way forward."

Fion pointed to Hunter. "Unless we put his head on a pike, there is no way forward."

"Perhaps separation is not so bad?" I asked.

Warin glanced at me.

"How so?"

I shrugged. "We can move faster. Cover more ground. Ophir." I pointed towards the mystic. "I think he knows more about this land than any of us. Maybe he knows a way to shut the cracks, to get out of this without throwing ourselves as the largest creature we can find. Surely, I am not the only one that finds that mad."

Fion laughed and spread his arms wide. "This land is mad, friend."

I shook my head. "Fighting will solve nothing."

Fion smiled and turned away.

"Strange words for a knight."

"Yet true."

Fion shrugged. "I don't think we see eye to eye on that, friend."

"No," I said. "Perhaps not."

I placed my hands against my head.

"Here's what I know," I said. "What we—"

Shapes moved in my peripheral. Things that shouldn't be there. I turned and saw Ophir was on his knees and Cornelius shouted, white light blazed from his hands. More shapes moved to my left, but I did not have time to look at them.

My sword was in my hand as I raced forward. Humanoid creatures with pale naked bodies and twisted faces grabbed at the confessor. He held his palm out as a blaze of white light shot forward, incinerating the nearest creature.

More poured out from the drop off. I raced towards the nearest one. I looked at its twisted face. It had two large black eyes that looked like they'd be more at home on a fly than a man. I swung, and the abomination went flailing to the ground.

Two more rushed around the first, reaching out grasping hands for me. I swung, severed both arms of one, but the other fell against me, reaching for my face. I twisted and broke free of the creature's gasp. Three more rushed in on me.

I brought my pommel up, no time to get my sword around for a proper strike and cracked the underside of the first creature's jaw. It sank to the floor as the other two grabbed at my sword. I turned back and forth, trying to break free.

A third creature ran around the first two, its arms flailed this way and that. Its large soulless eyes locked on me and it charged. It crashed into me. The force knocked me back, the other two yanked the sword from my hands.

I fell onto my back. The creature's icy fingers reached for my mouth and eyes. My hands shot up, knocking it back. I saw a flash of steel and cold blood sprayed down on me. I felt a hand on my shoulder, pulling me up.

Someone brought me to my feet, and I yanked my knife from my side. I waded forward, sliced wherever I saw exposed flesh. I tore through the creature that had knocked me down and engaged with the two that had taken my sword.

One demon's face contorted in on itself, giving it the appearance of an unnatural flower. The other had the eyes of a fly and it held my sword. It took a clumsy swing at me. I batted the sword aside and fell in, slamming my knife into the creature's stomach again and again until it fell.

The other ran forward, I plucked up my sword. I swung and decapitated the creature. I glanced around, searching for more enemies. The others ran towards me, a pile of bodies around us.

Then I saw Sacha. He clutched his face, blood ran between his fingers. He moaned. From my right, Alexei exploded from a pile of bodies. He rushed towards his brother, nearly knocking him over as he reached him.

"Sacha," said Alexei.

Sacha removed his bloody hands from his face, ribbons of flesh hung off. One eye was blood red, and the other was bloodshot. Matthew pushed his way between the onlookers. I saw the priest had red marks across his neck.

His hand glowed white, and he smacked it against Sacha's face.

"Pain is temporary," said Matthew in a sweet, calm voice.

Sacha looked up at him in confusion.

Then the pain started. Sacha screamed as the light consumed his face.

"Hold brother, please hold," said Matthew, steadying Sacha with one hand as he drove his glowing palm to his face.

Alexei held his brother tight.

"It's for healing, brother," said Alexei.

Sacha screamed again and fell forward. Matthew sank down with him, keeping his palm pressed against the poor boy. I glanced around. Fion's neck bled. Warin had a gash across his eye, making it close.

Ophir leaned on his staff, panting, with his left boot held off the ground as if he had a broken ankle. Blood covered Hunter's face, and he appeared severely bruised, as if he was halfway to death. Alexei had a growing bruise on his forehead.

Only Cornelius seemed unharmed. Around the confessor was smoking flesh.

Matthew pulled his hand from Sacha's face. The bleeding had stopped, but half of his face would have terrible scars. Matthew removed a kit from his side and pulled out a needle and string.

"Be still," he said to Sacha.

Alexei held his brother as Matthew threaded Sacha's face closed. I looked away. Warin stared at Sacha.

I glanced around. There were twelve, maybe thirteen, bodies of the creatures around us.

"They were weak," said Cornelius, shock in his voice.

I turned to the confessor. He was staring around wide eyed.

"Frail demons. Barely a dozen of them."

He looked up and locked eyes with me.

"And they almost killed us."

In that moment, I lost whatever hope I had clung to.

Chapter 18

"There is a way back...I think."

Hunter stood, staring at the ground. His body quivered. It hadn't stopped since we helped him to his feet and treated his wounds. His mouth had swollen, and a great welt had formed on his head.

Matthew had wrapped a bandage around his torn neck, which was now wet with blood. He looked around at the group.

"I think I can get us back," he repeated.

Matthew nodded. "We can't stay here." He held his hand out to one of the slain creatures. "These things were nothing but peons in this place and they almost slew us."

Matthew shook his head. "What hope do we have against the great enemies out there?"

Alexei and Sacha went and stood by Matthew.

"I agree with Matthew," said Alexei. "The risk of staying is too great. The council must have other ways of closing the gaps."

I looked up at the sky, at the cracks. If anything, they seemed to have grown stronger since we had arrived. I looked down at the still smoldering bodies.

Maybe the council was wrong. Maybe slaying empowered the creatures, not defeated them. A sickness twisted in my stomach, mixing with anger. If Septimus had sent us here on incomplete knowledge, risked our lives, I'd kill him upon my return.

"Weakness is a sin." Cornelius strode forward, eyeing Matthew and Hunter in particular.

"If we flee now, what do you think will happen?" asked Cornelius. "Do you think the cracks will go away, that the attacks will lessen? Hmm? What do you think happens to your homes?"

Cornelius snapped to Hunter.

"As a lowly drunk, you may not have friends, family, or anyone that cares about you. But we all do. We all have those we cherish back home. And because of this, we cannot sit around and drink ourselves blind while the world burns around us."

"I have loved ones," said Hunter.

Cornelius scoffed.

Warin stepped forward. "Cornelius is right…in a way. If we don't confront this now. If we do not solve this now. It will only get worse. The cracks will not stop until they consume our entire world and leave nothing behind…until our world matches theirs."

The thought sent a chill through my heart. I imagined those creatures grabbing Erwin and Josephine. Tearing out their eyes and dragging them off to some horrible fate. It made me want to puke.

"The council," said Hunter. "The council will know what to do."

"The council is out of options," said Warin. "If they had any others, they would have used them. Breaching is the last option."

"How do you know that, though?" asked Hunter.

"Why do we listen to this lying coward's words?" asked Cornelius.

"Hold," said Warin, "Let him speak."

Hunter nodded. "How do we know the council is not lying to us? They have lied before. They lied to me. That's why I'm here."

"The council did not lie to you," said Cornelius.

"The council would not waste the sacred blood without grave concern," said Warin. "Such a rare artifact is not something they take lightly."

"Though you wasted it," said Cornelius, glaring at Hunter.

"Put a stopper in your hate, Cornelius," said Matthew. "The poor man did what he thought was best."

"And look where that got us."

The two holy men faced off against one another. Warin held a hand to his temple and shook his head.

Sacha stepped forward. "What is the purpose of this? We did our best, and it was not enough. So we return home. Where is the harm in that? We can fight the demons on the other side. The other side where we have armies at our backs."

"We must stay here," said Ophir. "There are things here that we cannot leave."

"Why?" asked Sacha. "If we will just die?"

"They surprised us," said Fion. "We let our guard down and suffered the consequences."

"It won't matter when we face a giant," said Sacha. "It won't matter how close we are then."

I swiped my hand across my face. The bickering was getting nowhere and threatened to flay the last of my nerves. I walked off a few paces as the discussion went back and forth.

I thought about going home, about seeing my family again, holding Josephine and Erwin, something that seemed further and further away the longer I was in this land.

Sure, the cracks would widen, and this world would storm through, and our armies would not best it. They would fight valiantly, I'm sure. But the horrors of this world were endless. After a few years, our world would lose, and the fallen kingdom would emerge victorious.

Erwin and Josephine, along with the rest of humanity, would meet fates worse than death. Unless...unless the armies could withstand the onslaught. Maybe long enough to have a brief life with them.

I wiped my neck so hard it hurt. I dropped my hand to my side and turned back to the others. Cornelius and Matthew traded another round of insults.

"Hold," I said, stepping into the mix.

All eyes turned to me.

"Hunter, where do we go home at?"

Hunter looked up; a smile crossed his face. I heard a gasp from someone behind me.

"I...I remember little. But it's not out here. We must get into the walls. We get in there and there should be certain....places that can bring us home. That council said something about that...I remember"

"Alright," I said. "Then that's what we do."

"Knight, you are not in charge of this," said Cornelius.

The confessor's tone made my blood boil. I whirled on him.

"And you are confessor?"

"Alaric," said Warin.

The confessor locked eyes with me. I saw a passionate blaze there. We stared at each other for a few moments. I turned back to the group.

"On our way there, if we come across a demon worth slaying, then we slay it and see if that has any effect on the cracks."

"Do you doubt the council's word?" asked Matthew.

I saw concern on his face.

"Breaches have been successful in the past," said Cornelius. "You of all people, knight, should know of Aldin the Unchallenged, and the many others who went before. You served at the Survivor's Ball, did you not?'

"I did," I said, turning to Cornelius. "And I know the destruction that I saw there. That we both did."

I glanced at Fion. His eyes were wide, he remembered that night. Mangled survivors. Men we thought heroes that were in fact tortured ghosts.

I looked at Cornelius. "Finding an exit is not the worst thing."

"That's where you're wrong." Cornelius glared at me. "When Harold the Conqueror landed on the shores of Tremoli. He was successful with such a small force for one reason and one reason only. He burned his ships, cutting off any other option. Victory or death were the only options allowed."

Cornelius looked around at the group.

"Give us a way out. A way to let our weakness and frailness prevail, and we shall never make it. The fallen world requires all of a man, if he is to succeed. Half measures will be our deaths."

"He has a point," said Warin. "And I need not remind you, Alaric. Failure here means failure back home."

"Can they not send more after us?" I asked.

Fion looked at me like I had said the knights were all fools and I regretted ever becoming one.

"Alaric..." said Warin, staring at me. "There is not time and even if there were, such thoughts will lead to death. Cornelius is right, no half measures."

"I want to live!" Hunter screamed.

I turned as he shot forward for Cornelius.

"Wait," I shouted, running for Hunter.

I grabbed his ax hand as Matthew grabbed his arm. We wrestled him back. I looked over my shoulder and saw a light blazed at the end of Cornelius' mace.

"Come to your judgement, fool," said Cornelius.

"Wait," I said, holding up my hand.

Others had advanced. The entire group seemed ready to war with one another, all except Warin.

Warin stepped forward in front of Cornelius and placed a hand on the front of the man's robes.

"Hold."

He pushed Cornelius back. I grabbed Hunter and pulled him up, looking around at the group.

If things continued this way, we would not make it off this path. Much less have any chance of getting home or closing the gaps.

And saving those back home.

Chapter 19

Death.

That's what waited for us. We were separated again. We had nearly died from being separated not a few moments prior and now here we were again. I had to do something. We would never survive in this land if we were going to be at each other's throats.

I looked at Warin. He stood next to Fion, his face was pinched, worried, and I did not blame him. He seemed to recede from everything around him, like he was drawn into himself, resigning himself to whatever fate lay in store for us.

I had seen in before in him and I'd consider it his only weakness. I walked towards him. Fion glanced at me, but Warin remained lost in his trace.

"Brother, master."

Both turned to me.

"We have a problem," I said.

"We have many problems," replied Fion.

"We cannot sit here, bickering, not moving. We should at least bicker while we move. At least that would accomplish something."

"We can't go home, Alaric," said Fion, "What are we going home to? Homes that will soon face destruction? Families that will soon face slaughter?"

I had given up the delusion that our armies could hold back the tides of horror. Breaching had become common practice because we all knew the armies would fail against the endless tide. Only the closing of the cracks could save home.

"I know."

Both my companions seemed surprised.

"But that doesn't change the fact that I think we should identify a way out of here. And that doesn't change the fact that I want to go home and it doesn't change the fact that I think fighting these things will only make things worse."

I took a deep breath.

"But regardless of what path we take forward, we must do it together. Otherwise, we might as well throw ourselves off the cliff side now."

"What do you propose?" asked Warin.

"What do you want, Warin?" I asked.

"What?"

"What do you want?"

"What do I want?"

Warin's brows narrowed. I could see his mind turned something over.

"I want to complete the mission."

"And what is the best way to do that?" I asked.

"Cornelius already said it. He may not have a way with words, but he speaks the truth." Warin looked at me. "Find the demons with the most power, slay them. That will weaken and eventually destroy the cracks."

"We cannot do that without all of us together," I said.

"No," said Fion. "But some help more than others."

"We need everyone right now," I said. I let out a sigh. "I want to go back home. I want to see them again."

My voice cracked. Fion looked down and Warin's eyes softened.

"I know, Alaric. I know what you want."

I looked at the group.

"We all want the same thing here. There's no reason we should all be fighting."

I walked towards Cornelius.

He stood with Alexei and Sacha. Alexei looked up as I neared. Cornelius spun as if he was about to be attacked. Seeing me, his stance softened, but only a little.

"Knight," said Cornelius.

"Confessor," I replied. "I've come to talk with you."

"So speak."

"We don't have time for this."

Cornelius' eyes narrowed. "Time for what?"

"For this." I held up my hand, indicating around me.

"Then kill Hunter and let's be on with it."

"No."

Cornelius frowned.

"Him being alive is better for the group. He is one more that can fight and he's the only one that has been in this land before. Even if he has lied about some things."

"Justice must be served."

"And it will be, but what about justice for our people? Justice for our world back home?"

"What do you mean?"

Cornelius turned to face me in full.

"We sit here and bicker, meanwhile demons come into our world. While we argue, demons can slaughter families, raze villages, and scour our lands."

Alexei's eyes widened behind Cornelius.

"There are things more important than Hunter. Survival for one. Destruction of powerful demons for another. Let Hunter come with us. After we slay the demons and close the cracks, then we can bring him to whatever justice he deserves."

Cornelius held a finger to his chin. "I think our disagreement stems deeper than this. I said before and I'll say again, half measures will destroy us."

"So damn the half measures," I said.

"How?" asked Cornelius.

"We will need to find a way home anyway. We all want to get out of this place. Right now, we go where the strongest demons are, and then we work from there, together, as a team."

Cornelius didn't seem convinced.

"We all want the same thing here. We all want to save our home and destroy the demons."

I let my voice carry so that the others could hear it.

"Then let's do that. We can worry about petty squabbles after the cracks are closed, not before."

"So long as we do not strive to find home first, but fulfill our mission first, as the council intended, do I agree to this," said Cornelius.

I turned and nodded to Matthew.

"They'll let Hunter live. But he will be required to fight."

"I can do that," said Hunter. "I can fight. There is no concern there."

I nodded and looked around. The separate groups were all moving towards me, spiraling around me.

"Our mission is clear."

I locked eyes with Warin.

"We stand together. We go into the walls. We slay the strongest demons that we can find. It is our responsibility to seal the cracks. Then we go home. Then, and only then, do we worry about the things that divide us. Then, and only then, do we worry about other matters. Is that understood?"

The group spoke as one.

"Understood."

We were ready to move out.

Chapter 20

We found our way into the city proper. Hunter led us towards the drop off to a thin staircase that descended into foggy depths. We went down, and up the other side, into the city proper.

I gawked at the towering buildings around us. Their once gold sides gleamed with a sickly green light. The fog roiled overhead, many of the buildings' tops were lost in its depths.

There was something else.

I had said nothing, but ever since we had walked beyond the wall, I felt something. Something dark pressed down on me. A presence. Ever since we emerged from the fog, I felt it. We walked towards the center of the city; the buildings blocked the view of what lay ahead.

I glanced up at a nearby building. The building flaunted polished stone construction, with ornate carvings of ancient heroes running down the side. I had heard many rumors of the splendor of the fallen world, of times before the fall, but seeing it was another thing entirely.

Two great arched doors led into the building. One was open. Fog seeped out from inside. I looked up and saw a steeple high above. I looked at Warin, he gawked at the architecture as well.

The city was beautiful, even in decay.

Ophir walked ahead. A low, thin fog hung across the street in front of us. Ophir stamped his staff on the cobbles and a blue light illuminated the ground ahead. Cornelius held up his mace and a white light shone from it.

We entered the fog, following the two lights. We emerged onto an overlook that looked out over an impossible land. Far away, the other side of the wall stretched high into the sky. Between us and the other wall was an entire world.

I saw forests, the mist seeping off the trees. Castles, cities, great plains, burned fields, and rocky slopes. The fallen kingdom lay before us. My eyes roved through the landscape, tried to make out unnatural shapes or creatures.

I had heard that demons the size of homes roamed these lands but saw nothing. They either knew to hide themselves or the stories were lies.

Though they'd have little reason to hide from us.

"It's beautiful," said Sacha.

Sacha walked to the edge of the overlook.

"Careful, brother," said Alexei.

Sacha nodded, but he couldn't take his eyes off the world before him. The boy looked close to tears.

"It's so beautiful," he said again.

"It's what we once were," said Warin. "Before the fall."

"We've lost so much," said Sacha.

Cornelius looked around, like something bothered him. Our eyes met for a moment. He frowned and looked away. Ophir stood next to Sacha with a hand on his shoulder.

"There are great mysteries in these lands," said Ophir. "Great mysteries just waiting to be discovered. Things that could change our world back home, things that could change everything."

Sacha looked at Ophir, then back out at the vista. Fion stood next to me.

"Something feels off," he whispered. "I know you feel it. I can sense your unease, brother."

I nodded. "So it does."

"Don't ignore that," replied Fion. "A warrior's gut will not lead him wrong."

"Your gut is always telling you there's trouble."

"And I am seldom wrong," replied Fion, he looked at me with an eyebrow raised.

I shook my head and studied my companions. Matthew, for once, seemed unnerved. He was not speaking, but had his arms folded tight across his chest. Warin gazed, lost in the vista. Hunter leaned forward; his eyes glazed over.

"Do you not feel it?" asked Matthew.

All eyes turned to the monk.

"Matthew," said Warin. "Maybe it's best not to speak about such things."

"You all feel it too then?" asked Sacha. "I thought I was the only one."

"We all feel it," replied Hunter, still staring at the floor. "The presence coats the air in this cursed place."

"Presence of what?" asked Matthew.

"The demons., replied Hunter. "What else?"

"Then we are in the right place," I said.

Hunter laughed. His laugh sent a chill down my spine.

"We'll see, knight," he said, rocking back and forth. "We'll see."

Cornelius looked at me as if to say 'I told you so'. I didn't meet his eyes. Cornelius spoke.

"Their taint affects us all. We must stay vigilant. They are near, which means our goal is near."

"Does anyone not feel anything?" asked Sacha, glancing around, his eyes wide.

Alexei shrugged. "I feel no more uneasy than I did when we first entered this land."

"Anyone else?" asked Sacha.

No one answered.

"When did we all first feel it?" asked Sacha.

"When we entered the city." Said Matthew.

Sacha nodded. "That's when I felt it too."

The fear that was in my gut grew, made its way towards my heart.

"So we are not alone," said Fion.

"We were never alone," said Warin. "But we will be fine. So long as we stay together."

Hunter laughed.

"Silence, Hunter." Cornelius' words were laced with threat. He spoke low, "Or I shall do it for you."

"It doesn't matter," whispered Hunter.

Hunter had changed more than the others since we entered the city. Like a man that had given up the last of his hope. He seemed dangerous, a potential liability. Part of me wondered if handing him over to Cornelius might be the right choice.

"Hunter," said Ophir. "Do you know the way forward?"

The mystic was eager to make progress. I could not blame him for that.

"I don't know the way," replied Hunter. "I know nothing. We should get out of here."

"Hunter," said Matthew, walking towards the man. "Hold it together, friend." Matthew's voice was soft. "You are our guide. We believe in you. You got us here."

Hunter smiled his mirthless smile.

"I've doomed us all."

"Enough of that," I said.

Hunter made the presence feel worse. He put me on edge. And we needed to stay calm.

"What's the way forward, Hunter?"

"Follow the presence," replied Hunter. "The demons leave their snares in plain sight. If we're fool enough to follow, they will find us."

The presence seemed to grow.

"We are not alone here," said Sacha, his eyes roamed the buildings.

"Of course not, brother," said Alexei. "We were never alone here, that is the point. We came here to slay demons."

I could not tell if Alexei didn't realize his brother did not ask a literal question or not.

Part of me was impressed by Alexei. All of us felt the darkness. Some of us were close to madness. And he stood in the middle of it all as if he stood in line at tournament. While I could see there was some concern on his face, it seemed to be for Sacha. He seemed fine himself.

I envied him.

I cleared my throat. "We just need to stick—"

A loud crash echoed out from behind me. I dove forward, tripped and nearly rolled off the edge of the overlook. I whirled.

More crashing sounds. The walls of a nearby building fell, sending up dust.

Something stirred within the debris.

"We need to move!" shouted Ophir.

I whirled and saw the mystic disappear off the side of the lookout. I rushed over and saw he took a steep path down into the forest below. Others rushed away. I looked back at the falling building. Another wall came tumbling down, and a screech echoed out from the debris.

That was enough.

I turned to follow Ophir when I realized half the party had scattered in another direction. Sacha, Matthew, Hunter, and Alexei had run back towards the city.

I sprinted for them.

I reached them as they huddled among the wreckage.

"Come on. This isn't the place to stay. We need to stick together," I said.

Another wall came tumbling down, and the inhuman shrieks resumed. We tore across the overlook and down the steep path. Doing our best to ignore whatever transpired behind us.

I glanced down the path and saw no sign of Warin or the others.

And my heart dropped.

Chapter 21

We followed a path that led through a small forest and to a bridge that spanned the greater forest below us. The fog covered the greater forest, with only the tree tops visible.

The bridge was beautiful, though decayed. Parts had broken away and ivy climbed up the supports. The cobbles had cracked and much of the siding had broken off and slid into the forest below.

Far away, I could make out a few forms on the bridge. I saw the gleam of armor and knew it was Warin and the others.

"Come, we're close," I said.

I heard shouting from the other side of the bridge. I looked up. Cornelius waved a hand over his head. We made our way across. The bridge was wide enough for five or six carriages.

It made me think of the grandeur of this place. Of how much had been lost to the demons. I had heard many stories of the time before the fall. Before mankind's acceptance and eventual defense of the demons. The demons that almost wiped us out.

The surrounding land was a potent reminder of the foolishness of man.

We neared the other group. Cornelius walked over, smiling.

"We have found something," he said.

"Found something?" I asked. "What?"

"Evidence of a wounded demon. A powerful one," said Warin.

"A wounded demon?" I asked.

"Come," said Fion.

We raced across the bridge. On the other side was a dirt path that led into a darkened wood. We ran up the path and to another part of the ruined city.

"Here." Cornelius pointed off the side of the trail.

I noticed bark torn away in sheets from a few trees. A black ichor stained the lower parts of the trees, still wet.

Cornelius pointed up the trail. I followed the black ichor up into another part of the city.

"Still wet," said Cornelius.

He had a gleam in his eyes when he said the word. I felt slaying demons to him was akin to making love to a beautiful woman for other men.

"Come," said Cornelius.

We followed the trail of black ichor up into another part of the city. Tall buildings crowded in on either side, leading us down a road. The road took a sharp left turn, and we followed.

And there I saw my first great demon.

The road led out to a smaller path that led to a circular landing. It stood out over a cliff face, an observatory of sorts. Whatever railing had been in place was gone, leaving a circle of stone out over a large drop into the forest below.

In that circle rested a strange beast. Its torso was wide and covered with armor. It sat on its side like a cat or dog. It tucked its hind legs underneath it, also armored, while splaying out its forearms in front of it.

It had an elongated neck, its head covered with a helm. Two blue eyes glinted from the eye slots in the helm.

The creature struggled to breathe, it was close to death.

"What luck," said Cornelius, clapping his hands together.

"Stay cautious," said Warin. "We have to be careful, and we have to stick together."

I don't know why, but hearing Warin say that made me uneasy. How easy it was to get separated, how fast that could lead to one's destruction.

We advanced as a party. We stopped at the short walkway that led out to the circular landing. The creature stared at us but made no move to defend itself. Cornelius had his mace out, the head glowed bright white.

"How do we approach this?" asked Fion.

Ophir stepped forward.

"Sacha, come by my side," said Ophir.

Sacha walked up next to Ophir and took out his wand.

"Cornelius, you as well. Alexei, do you have the power?" asked Ophir.

"Faint, not like my brother," said Alexei. "But it is there."

The four stood in line.

"We will use what we must slay the creature. Knights, be ready if the creature moves, though I feel it is beyond that," said Ophir.

I nodded and glanced at Warin. I was unsure what Ophir was going to do, and Warin seemed just as confused as me. Warin waved me over.

"Let's be ready."

The rest of us drew our weapons and stood to the side. Each of the four men channeled their powers. Ophir held out his staff, and three glowing blue orbs formed above him.

Sacha did likewise and formed a single glowing blue orb above his head. Alexei tried but seemed to fail, his sword a poor channeler.

Cornelius channeled an orb of white light that he held in his hands. His face was twisted as if the orb pained him.

"Unleash," said Ophir.

I watched the orbs sail through the air and slam against the creature. They twisted and tore at the metal covering the creature's skin. The creature let out a long, mournful groan that sounded too close to human to be comfortable.

I looked at the massive brute. Its torso stretched the length of the four men arrayed against it. Something like this could never have been human, or at least that's what I had to believe.

The men began their channeling again. Alexei channeled a sliver of the blue energy. They shot the energy forward, and it slammed into the creature again. The creature bucked up, as if about to rise.

I turned with my sword raised, not sure what I could do against something so large.

The creature let another, too close to human, moan. Its great voice echoed across the city and the forest below. And then it collapsed, showing its belly to us.

Armor covered the creature's underside. I noticed the creature had two humanlike arms that ended in gauntleted hands.

I let my sword drop from in front of me, breathing out a sigh of relief. I heard a creak and looked up. Though I couldn't be certain, I thought I saw a warp through the cracks.

I glanced at Warin.

"Did you see that?"

Warin nodded.

"Something changed up there."

I let out a nervous laugh. I glanced at Fion. His mouth was open at what he had just seen.

"Did you hear that?" asked Cornelius, sounding like a kid who had received a brand new sword.

"The cracks," said Matthew. "They changed. I saw it."

Cornelius and Matthew looked at each for a moment, for the first time without animosity.

"It changed," said Fion. "I saw it clearly. Something changed."

I smiled. It felt good.

No, it felt great.

We had acted, and it had changed. Warping the cracks didn't eliminate them, but when I looked up, they seemed less powerful. They seemed less bright, less wide.

I knew there was still much work to be done.

Through the slaying of the demon, our world was one step closer to being safe. My family was one step closer to being safe. And I was one step closer to going home.

Joy shot through me. I leapt in the air, something I had not done since I was a boy. I turned to Fion and we slammed into each other, embracing and slapping each other on the back.

Warin laughed.

"That was the first," said Warin. "Take time to rejoice but—"

A loud echoing screech sent all of us scrambling to our knees, hands clamped to our ears. A colossal form rose from the forest below. It had the head of a dragon and long arms ending in claws.

It roared, parts of its face splitting revealing alien mouths. A great claw came hurtling through the air at us. The claws were so large it seemed as if moving through water.

I turned and fled. The impact of the claw sent me soaring through the air. For a moment, my vision was clear, and I could see everything. The impossible sized demon, my companions scattered through the sky, and the complete and utter destruction of the landing we were on.

All that and the futility of all that we sought to accomplish here.

I fell further than I should have. It was then I realized I had not made it back to the city street but was falling into the forest below. Someone hit above me, landing on the city street.

But I descended into the fog.

And I knew I would soon die.

Chapter 22

The fall was less painful than I expected. I crashed against tree branches, twisting this way and that. I slammed against the ground. It knocked the wind out of me. I spent a good minute curled up in a ball, trying to take a breath.

My sword had clattered close by, giving me some measure of comfort. When my lungs worked again, I uncurled myself and looked around. I could make out tall trees around me, but that was it. The fog was dense, its weight like a living presence.

I stood up, taking my time. I felt no pain, but it gave me little comfort. Perhaps something had broken that couldn't be fixed, and my body was in a state of numbness. I stood to my full height and patted my body. I felt a few bruises, and when I stretched, my back ached. But other than that, I was fine.

I heard a great thundering sound that grew more distant. I glanced up, tried to make out where the landing had been, but I couldn't see the top of the tree I crashed against. I grabbed my sword and stared at the mist covered land before me, not sure what to do.

Sounds echoed to me from the wood. Strange cooing sounds followed by cracking branches. My stomach tensed up, I forced myself forward. I looked back and forth with every step I took, my nerves tensed at every sound that came from the forest.

I studied the ground and saw that I was on a ragged old path. The grass was bent, and I saw stones here and there. Ahead of me was nothing but the dense fog. I thought about shouting, about seeing if any of the others were close by. But the last thing I wanted to do was draw attention to myself.

I continued down the path until I came to a fork. One path trailed off to my left and another to my right. Before me was a tall statue on a pedestal. I looked up at the statue. A grand horse reared back, made of a white marble with black lacing.

I imagined myself in what were once beautiful gardens. I stared at the statue, admired its beauty. Then I heard something in the woods to my right. I spun, my back tightening, and raised my sword.

I saw a faint light down the path. A blue light. I lowered my sword. The light stopped and moved away. I moved after it.

The light had to be Ophir, or if not Ophir, then Sacha. I bit my lip to keep myself from calling out. I followed the light, like a moth to a flame.

I hated being alone in this land, without the others next to me. The blue light got fainter. Panic gnawed at me.

"Hey!" I yelled into the fog.

No sooner had the words left my mouth than I smacked a hand to my lips.

The blue light stopped. I stood still as the light moved closer to me.

Had I just killed myself?

I brought my sword up.

"Ophir?" I asked.

The light continued to move towards me, but I heard no response.

"Sacha?" I asked, my voice soft.

The fog parted, and I saw a large conical hat.

"Ophir."

I raced towards the man. Ophir looked up, and I grabbed him and crushed him to me. I let go and looked down at the mystic.

He stared at me, frowning.

"I'm sorry," I said. "Being alone in this land…it gets hard to keep the madness at bay."

Ophir nodded. He glanced around, then spotted the statue. His eyes widened, and he pushed past me.

"I can't believe you're alive," I said. "That was a great fall for all of us."

"You're alive, aren't you?"

Ophir stopped in front of the statue, looked it up and down.

"Did you see others?"

Ophir turned on his heels and looked at me.

"You need to listen to me. There are things I can sense in this land. I can lead you to where we need to go."

"Did you see any others?" I asked.

Ophir frowned.

"It may just be me and you now, knight. We must take care. Come, with your sword and my magic. We can carve our way through this land and get to where we must go."

"You know the way forward?" I asked.

There was a fervor in Ophir's voice that would have been unnerving under different circumstances.

"I do."

Ophir turned and went down the left-hand path.

"You still didn't tell," I asked. "Did any of the others survive?"

"No one survived that knight," said Ophir. "Who knows, maybe me and you are dead right now."

I glanced back at where the landing would have been. Maybe he was right, maybe we had died.

I thought of Warin and Fion, my heart twisted for them. I took a step away from Ophir, back towards where we had all fallen.

"Where are you going?" asked Ophir.

"The others…" I started. "Maybe some of them still live. They could be in the forest."

"No one lives down here with us," said Ophir. "There is no natural life in this forest. Perhaps a few are still alive in the city proper, and if so we may rejoin with them at a later time."

I felt a light hand on my shoulder. I turned and saw Ophir stared at me.

"For now, we have a task ahead of us."

"Task? To slay the demons? Just me and you?"

"Follow me." Ophir turned and waved for me to follow.

"I will show you great mysteries, knight. Great power we can use to do whatever we will. The ancient ways are before us, closer than ever."

I shook my head. "I don't know what you speak of, Ophir. We must make sure the others are okay. That they're safe. We cannot complete this quest alone."

"Alaric," said Ophir, using my name for the first time. "There are things beyond your understanding in this world. Whoever lives, we will reunite with them. For now, we have a path before us, and we must take it."

I nodded. My heart twisted. I didn't want to leave this spot. The probability of others falling without injury was slim, I knew. I knew there were those in our party that now lay dead somewhere around or above me.

The mystic's words soothed me. Of anyone, he would know the secret ways of this land and perhaps a way to save the quest.

"Alright," I said. "Lead the way."

Chapter 23

Ophir seemed to know where he was going. He moved through the fog like a hound on a scent. I kept close behind him. Strange sounds echoed around us as we moved. A few times I thought I heard a child crying, another time, the whisperings of a woman. Once, I thought I heard Warin call my name.

Ophir said to give it no mind, so we continued. Soon, the mist parted, and we walked out into a lower section of the city. The buildings here were older. The tarnished golds of the city above gave way to dark stones worn by time, stones of ancient castles and defenses, not of a glittering golden age.

I glanced back at the fog covered forest, wondering if it contained the others, wondering if we would ever see them again.

"Do not lag," said Ophir.

I nodded and kept up with the mystic. Ahead of us were the ruins of an ancient fort that overlooked a substantial drop off. I could not see what lay below the drop off, but I thought I heard the lapping of water.

We walked towards the fort. It looked as if a giant had attacked and torn down one side of the decrepit stronghold. The wall crumbled off the side of the drop off. I shivered as we neared.

"You have nothing to fear," said Ophir. "I am leading us to a great thing, knight."

"A great thing?" I asked.

The mystic acted weird, though I could not tell if that was who he was or if something had happened to him in the fall. I knew we were all close to madness in this land and that genius and madness lay close to one another. If I wasn't such a doddering fool, I may have gone mad already.

Ophir leaned on his staff as he worked his way to the fort, as if it pained him to move.

"Do you want to rest, Ophir?" I asked.

"Rest?" asked the mystic. "In this land? Are you mad?"

"You seemed pained."

Ophir shook his head.

"It's nothing. We need to make better time."

With this, he moved faster.

We neared the front of the fort. Most of an old draw bridge lay decayed in a small stream below. At one point, it looked like a river had flown through here, but it made little sense. The river would have only stretched a stone's throw in either direction, each side ending at the drop off.

Ophir was at the start of what was left of the draw bridge. He poked at the blackened wood with his staff.

"That doesn't look safe," I said.

"Nothing here is safe," replied Ophir. "That is why we seek knowledge, to drive out the darkness."

I looked at the fort beyond Ophir. It was an ancient thing. Square and made of wood. The fort was scarred along its sides, as if it had seen many a battle.

Ophir started across a beam of the decayed drawbridge. I walked behind him. The fall was not too great. It would not kill me, but I could still end up with a twisted ankle or leg.

We crossed the drawbridge without event and made our way to the front of the fort. Two great doors led into the fort, both warped.

"There's power here," said Ophir. "Great power."

I shook my head; unease ate at me.

"We need to find the others."

Ophir waved a hand at me. "Worry not, knight. What is within these walls will give us all we need."

"What do you mean?" I asked.

Ophir walked up to one of the warped doors and yanked on it. He looked back at me.

"A little help, knight."

I walked up and together we opened the door enough to slip through. Inside, all the windows were closed, the only light came from behind us. Ophir's staff glowed blue, illuminating the room.

He walked towards the center and threw back a door there. I saw stairs that led down.

"Have you been here before?" I asked.

Ophir descended the stairs. "Never, but I know what I sense."

I followed him down the stairs. We navigated tight hallways until we reached a hole that led out onto the cliff side. A path stretched down to a shrine far below.

"We're here," said Ophir.

"Where?" I asked.

Worry gnawed at me. There was something here that was different. I felt off, like something was here with us, something dark. Something that pressed in on my heart. I looked at the cliff side a few steps from us. At the drop off that would plummet me to my death.

Jump, jump and free yourself.

The thought entered my mind unbidden. I clutched at my sword, the only place I could find comfort. I knew the thought was not my own. And that worried me. Ophir led me down to the shrine and then I saw what it was.

A statue of a black dragon sat on a small wall near the edge of the cliff. The statue looked so lifelike; it was hard to approach it. The mix of fear and madness I had felt earlier pressed down on me like an anvil.

Ophir walked to the statue. He swung his arms above his head and made a cackling laugh.

"Knight," he said. "Knight, we have found it."

"Found what, Ophir?" I asked.

He turned to me.

"Our salvation."

Chapter 24

Ophir knelt before the statue, his staff placed before him. The wrongness of the place was like a needle in my mind. I glanced around. This was the only path that led to this altar. I looked at the dragon.

It looked so lifelike. I expected at any moment for it to open its eyes and devour us whole. I looked at Ophir. The man possessed knowledge and wisdom that surpassed my understanding.

I understood the blade, but this magic was far beyond me. I looked at the dragon again. No doubt it held great power, but there was darkness to it. I knew little, but I knew this thing would not be our salvation.

I fidgeted, rocked my weight side to side, waited for Ophir to stir, to say something. To say it was all a misunderstanding and we needed to be on our way. To apologize for his temporary slide into madness and we'd find the others.

I went to a small wall the statue rested on. It was waist high. I leaned against it, looking out over the drop off. Fog blocked me from seeing far, but I had the impression I looked out over an ocean that stretched for leagues ahead.

I shook my head. Everything about this place seemed alien. It was a wonder that humans could ever have survived here. I sat, lost in my thoughts until the building dread was almost too much to bear.

"Ophir," I said.

The mystic did not answer.

"Ophir," I repeated.

The mystic sat with his eyes closed, lost in his trance. I pushed up from the wall and walked over to the mystic. I leaned down and set a hand on his shoulder. His eyes shot open. For a moment, it was like I stared into someone else's eyes.

Then the mystic returned.

He looked up.

"What have you disturbed me for, knight?"

"Ophir," I said, trying to keep my voice calm. "What is going on? You have sat here staring at this statue for half a day."

Though, of course, there was no way to tell accurate time in this stagnant world.

Ophir blinked, then narrowed his eyes.

"I have great work I am accomplishing here."

"We need to keep moving. To find the others if they still live, to complete our quest."

Ophir smiled, then laughed.

"Our noble quest?" Ophir grabbed his staff and struggled to his feet. I helped him up.

Once up, he looked at me.

"You think me and you alone will slay any grand demons? Alone, the dregs we encountered on the bridge would tear us to shreds. And you think we will slay great monsters?"

He had a point.

I sighed and shrugged.

"What are we doing here?"

Ophir nodded to the dragon.

"Channeling great power."

The dragon stared at me.

"Power? What power is there here?"

I could feel the power, but it was dark, nothing that would do us any good.

Ophir smiled, his eyes bored into mine.

"I know you feel the power."

"Of course."

I took a step back from the mystic and crossed my arms.

"Of course, I feel the power," I said. "You feel it too, but you know something is off about it, something is wrong."

Ophir held up a finger. "Only to our limited perceptions. The dragons." Ophir's face glowed as he spoke their name. "Were beings of immense power. Of terrible knowledge. As god is separate from man, so was dragon."

Ophir looked at the statue.

"So, of course, their power feels wrong to us, because it is beyond our feeble understanding. But," Ophir whirled and looked at me. "If we can unlock the immense power of the dragons, we'd be unstoppable. We'd have power unimaginable to us mortals. Though I don't expect a knight to understand what can be learned from a dragon."

I tried to let the barb slide, but it stuck like a thorn in my throat.

"The knights of old slew the dragons for their evil. Because they attempted to destroy man."

Ophir shook his head.

"The dragons were never wiped out."

I held up my hand.

"We're getting sidetracked." I looked at the awful statue. "That thing." I pointed at it. "Will not do us any good and staying here will only lead to madness."

My voice was strained. The presence of this place was getting to me. I needed to leave, I needed to leave and find the others.

"I'm going, Ophir. If we stay here, nothing good will happen."

Ophir sighed and shook his head. "The folly of youth. Very well, knight, I will not stop you from leaving." He locked eyes with me. "But listen to me. You will not find your friends out there, the only thing you will find is death. Here..." He pointed to the ground. "Here is where salvation lies."

"I think otherwise." I nodded to Ophir. "Best of luck, mystic."

"And to you as well, knight."

We gave each other a bow and went our separate ways. I climbed out of the fort, thinking about the impossibility of the task before me. I did not know where I would go, how large this impossible land was, if any of the companions had survived, or what chance I had of completing my quest and seeing Josephine and Erwin again.

I had made it to the front of the fort. Everything seemed to crash down on me. I stopped and sank to my knees. My breath came in shuddered gasps.

I would not see them again.

I would never get out.

I was going to die here, and the cracks would grow, and my family would die. Away from me, alone and scared.

And there was nothing I could do.

Rage flared inside in, pushed out the fear. I balled my hands into fists and struck the ground again and again. I watched as clods of dirt peeled away as I let out angered grunts. I shouted and raged, not caring what lie around me, what could hear me.

If death stalked me, as it always did in this land, so be it.

Because a man can only bear so much before he breaks. No matter the man, no matter his mettle.

My rage subsided, and I sat in an exhausted heap. The grass before me pulverized into a mess. I looked up. Ahead of me was the path leading back into that cursed forest. The fog never let me see far beyond that.

I longed for the view from overhead. When I could see vistas stretched before me, even if the vistas contained unknown horrors.

I leaned forward and set my head on the grass.

Then I heard a scream.

I shot up, thinking I had screamed. But it came from behind. I turned.

Ophir.

I shot down the path back towards the altar. The deeper I went, the more I could feel the dark essence of the altar pressing down on me. I heard more screams. Screams of pain. My sword was out as I rushed out onto the landing.

I stopped short, my breath caught in my chest. I saw Ophir.

He stood, stark naked. His robe and staff discarded by the wall. Blood dribbled from his arms and cheeks. Chunks of skin hung off his face. In his hands, he held an ebon knife dripping with blood.

"Ophir!" I shouted.

Ophir looked at me. One eye seemed to be the mystic I had known for a short time, while the other was a distinct presence. Something inhuman stared out. He smiled as he saw me.

"I've figured it out!" he shouted, sounding gleeful.

I lowered my sword and took a few steps towards him.

"What are you talking about?" I asked.

"The power! The source of power! Why we cannot understand it." He laughed at the last words. "I've finally found it."

He twirled, blood whipped from his arms and face as he did, his arms extended overhead.

"I've found it!"

"Ophir…what are you—"

He dug the knife into his cheek, carved off the skin and tore it from his face. He threw it to the ground where it landed with a wet flop that made my skin crawl. I tried to speak, but no words would come out.

"Scales!" screamed Ophir. "It's the scales that hold the power."

He laughed with joy.

"Now my power will be unlimited."

I turned away as he took the knife to himself again. I used my free hand to cover my ears as he threw the skin away like a soiled rag.

"Soon it will be complete," he said. "And I can channel their power."

I walked to the wall and looked over into the abyss. I had seen war, and I had seen terror. I had tossed my innards more than a few times, but this was something new to me. And my stomach wanted to reject it.

"Ophir," I said, refusing to look at him. "You're hurting yourself."

"I'm finding enlightenment, knight." His voice was labored.

I looked at him. At the skin hanging free from his face and arms. I shuddered.

"You're losing blood."

"And gaining power." He smiled and laughed.

I walked towards him. He brandished the knife towards me.

"Don't interfere, knight."

He sliced a chunk from his stomach. Blood pooled around his feet and streaked the landing. It always amazed me how much blood a single man could hold.

"Ophir…you'll die if you don't stop."

He was already dead. I just wanted him to stop.

Ophir responded by cutting into his chest. His face went taunt as he worked the knife across, his eyes wide. The skin removed; he ripped it free.

I took a step towards him. A blue light flashed in his hand.

"Do not stop my ascension."

I couldn't watch anymore.

I walked away. I heard Ophir collapse, mumbling as he did. I kept walking. I knew he was dead, and I knew there was nothing I could do. The presence of the place was too much to bear.

I had to leave. I had to flee.

I had to find the others.

I had to.

Chapter 25

How can a place have so much power? Everywhere I wandered, I could feel the weight of the cursed land weighing on me, dragging me down, sapping what vigor remained in my mind and body.

I wandered through the fog drenched forest, doing my best to avoid the sounds of roving monsters deeper in the wood. Whenever I heard something large, I went the other way.

I walked with one hand gripped tight to my sword. I came across grisly sights. I saw an opened hole, spikes sticking out of it. Decayed skeletons were impaled on the spikes from some age past.

Another place I saw two dead men back to back. They had died long ago, but the decay was slow in this land. Their faces were drawn and worn. The skin pulled tight against the bone. Their eyes had turned brown but had been undisturbed by animal or organism.

I left the men and ventured deeper into the wood. I followed the broken grass, hoping this path would lead me somewhere.

I noticed the trees were sparser, and then I entered a grassland. As a gust of wind blew, a vista unfolded before me. I stood close to another cliff, far below me, hilly grasslands stretched as far as I could see.

Mausoleums dotted the grassland. Small shapes circled the mausoleums here and there. I stared at the vastness of the land. I heard a moaning cry come from behind me and turned.

The fog drenched forest lay behind me. I had seen no sign of the others on my trek, and I realized I never would. I was alone in this land, and it would be up to me to finish the impossible task.

My knees grew weak. I fell against the soft grass. The grass was long and plush, comfortable to lie in. I rolled over and stared at the hazy sky. A twist in the grass close by made me shoot up. I turned with my sword drawn. Then I realized it was the wind. My nerves were on edge. I had to find a place to calm down.

The low moan echoed from the forest again.

I couldn't stay here. I must move. A path skirted the forest and went around a tall cliff face to my right. I followed the path. Despite there being a long drop off to my left and a sheer cliff face to my right, I felt safer on the path.

The fog became less dense, I found a certain comfort and even beauty in the rolling grasslands below. The proportions seemed off in this world. The grasslands had to stretch for leagues and leagues. Somewhere in the distance, I thought I saw another castle.

How big was this place? And how could we expect to make a dent in it? If this land stretched as far as a nation back home, then what would slaying a few demons here and there do?

I thought of Aldin the Unchallenged and how he had closed the cracks.

Which meant there was something we could do. After all the slaying of that poor brute on the landing had helped weaken the cracks. I rounded a corner, and I saw a welcome sight ahead of me.

Standing on a peninsula out over a misty drop off was a church. Memories flooded back to me of the church back home, of time spent with Josephine and Erwin, of feasts with my brother knights. I cried out upon seeing the structure.

It was a simple church, four stone walls and a steeple. Cracks laced the walls, and part of the roof had collapsed in. I ran towards it, stumbling across the grassy field.

I grabbed one of the two wooden doors leading in and yanked them open. They revealed an aisle that led to a small altar. Behind it was a painting of *The Suffering*. I pulled the door half shut behind me, keeping most of the place in darkness.

A sense of calm descended over me as I walked into the church, it was like one of my companions was with me. Madness seemed staved off, if only for a moment.

I walked to the altar and knelt before it. A worn chalice sat upon the altar. Behind it, underneath the painting of *The Suffering*, was a basin. I knelt before the altar and said my prayers. While I had never been a very religious man, the church was like finding a long-lost friend, as were the wonderful memories associated with it, the promise of something normal, to have some attachment to the Incarnate.

I knelt before the altar for hours. I didn't want to leave. I clung to the sense of calm, like a child to his mother.

I knew as soon as I left, the madness of this world would flood in and work into my mind. Worm its way inside until I ended up like Ophir.

I knew Ophir had a stronger mind than me, so what had happened to him unnerved me, more than I had thought at first. The mystic's madness kept repeating in my head. I had to clear those thoughts.

I turned with my back to the altar, stared at the door and the hostile world outside. I did not intend to leave the shelter. I didn't want to subject myself to the world out there.

I rested my head against the altar, sleep seemed impossible. I heard a shuffling that roused me. I sprung up and turned with my sword out. The shuffling came from near the basin, but I saw nothing.

"You won't take this place from me," I said. "You'll not have it. I'll fight you for it."

I backed outside the church. Once there, I snatched one door and yanked back, letting in the light. Then I grabbed the other and did the same. The interior of the church was lit up and I could see the basin.

I walked back in.

Then froze.

I had not been alone in the church. All along the walls were the flayed forms of humans. They were staked there by black and silver barbs. Their mouths sewn shut, and they all stared at me with eyes that were very much alive.

My sword clattered to the floor. How they lived defied understanding. Blood stained the walls behind them where they should have bled out years ago.

I glanced around at all the naked bodies and felt sick again. The poor souls all stared at me as I rocked forward. I ran to the nearest man and grabbed the barb.

His eyes widened as I grabbed the spike. I yanked the barb free and the man fell to the ground. He convulsed a few times, then lay still. I repeated this with two others before I discovered I was killing them.

There was no way to save them, and even the church was not safe.

I rushed outside and hurled onto the ground. Then I half crawled, half walked to the edge of the peninsula. I looked out over the enormous drop and screamed.

I screamed again and again and again.

My voice echoed across the emptiness. I took a deep breath to let out a thunderous roar when a deep bugling call echoed from the mists. I fell back. Whatever creature had made the sound, it was huge.

I crawled against the wall of the church and hung my head between my arms.

Alone, I was hopeless here.

Alone, I was already dead.

And alone I was.

Chapter 26

At some point, I knew I needed to move. Time moves differently in the fallen world. I looked up and it could have been days or hours, I was not sure. But I knew I had stayed in the same place for too long.

So I moved.

I traveled across the desolate land, my eyes half closed, stumbling here and there. It was like I became part of the land, just another lost denizen that would lose himself to madness.

I thought of Ophir, of his corpse that was no doubt still on the landing, the black dragon staring down at him. In a way, I envied him, as he had been liberated from this madness. He did not have death hanging over him like a sickle ready to descend.

I climbed up a wooded hill. The grass yellowed near the top and the trees were leafless. I placed my hand against a branch, and it snapped off, so dry it was.

I climbed to the top of the hill and sat in a small clearing. From my elevated position above the mist, I had a clearer view of the decrepit world around me. I saw the gap in the great wall where we had first entered. The twisted buildings of the city caught my eye. I saw the broken road where the landing had been torn off by the demon.

I saw the great cliff and knew on the other side of it was a fort and at the bottom of that fort, overlooking an endless sea, was the shrine of the dragon and the body of a former compatriot.

I saw the mist that filled the forest.

I could see everything.

My eyes roamed the vista. Somewhere out there were Fion and Warin, or at least their bodies. Somewhere out there was the rest of my party. The foolish lot that thought we could make a difference in this world. The foolish lot that thought we could best the demons.

My thoughts drifted back to Aldin the Unchallenged. A knight's thoughts often do when faced with challenge. How had he overcome this land? How had he bested these demons and done so alone?

I sat and pondered. I heard a screech sound out from the forest below. It sent a chill up my spine and stopped my thoughts short. I had to keep moving. There was an inexplicable feeling deep inside me urging me to keep moving.

I looked around at the brittle trees. I walked towards them. I went a short way down the hill when I came to a dried riverbed. Across from me, I heard movement. I looked up and saw a white wolf standing across the riverbed, staring at me.

Our eyes locked.

I saw something there I had yet to see in this land. I did not see madness or sickness in the wolf's eye. Something that chilled me deeper.

I saw humanity.

The wolf and I stared at each other for a few minutes. I glanced at the riverbank and reached down. I set my hand around a black rock. The wolf continued to stare at me. I raised my fist back to throw the rock and the wolf tensed.

It kept its eyes locked on mine. I lowered the rock and stared. The wolf turned and shot off into the wood. I followed it for a few seconds before I lost it in the fog.

I glanced at the rock in my hand. It was flint. With a heave, I tossed it up and caught it. I turned and walked back to the top of the hill to look out over the vista again. A deep loneliness welled up within me.

I longed to see another friendly face. I felt no hunger, no thirst, and I was not tired. What I wanted more than anything else was to not be alone in this world. To not have to face the task before me without someone at my back.

I turned to the middle of the hill, an idea growing in my mind. Death was preferable to being alone, which solidified what I had to do.

A few minutes later, I had a stack of wood gathered in the middle of the hill, with more stacked nearby. I sat down. I had my flint in one hand and a sharpened rock in the other. I looked down at my pile of rubble.

I struck the flint and saw sparks. I smiled.

Before long, I had a fire going. I knew I would attract attention, but I did not care. I turned to the wood and gathered more. I kept returning to add more dense logs.

Soon I had a blaze that reached high in the sky. I had to keep away from it, the heat was so intense. I watched as small bits of ember flitted through the air. I sighed and looked back.

The warmth left my body.

I had a host of watchers in the forest. Four of them. Long-limbed creatures, humanoid. I could almost see through them. Instead of faces they had oval shapes with smaller black ovals in the middle. They studied me and I felt menace.

I took a step back towards the fire, the heat uncomfortable but preferable to getting closer to the creatures in front of me. I couldn't do this alone. No man could, no knight, no mystic, no warrior, no poet, no priest, not anyone.

We were all tied to each other, and I was without them, which meant death had finally come for me. I held my sword up with one hand and pointed it towards the watchers.

A profound fear overcame me. My hand shook. I cleared my throat, and I sang. It was old song I had heard as a child with the knights, when they had first taken me to church. My voice was shaky, but I sang the words as best I could.

Come to me in this dark hour,

With my brethren far from me,

Lead my shaking hands to virtue,

That I may be blessed with Thee.

This I'll take and stand upon it.

Upon Thine guiding light.

I'll meet the darkness, stand against it.

For the sake of that I love.

The watchers crept closer. I took another step to the fire. The heat singed my back. My sword shook more. I gulped and cleared my throat.

Like a wisp among the shadows,

Like a sparrow far from home.

I'll stand athwart the darkness,

Knowing Your true love's hold.

Be with me in this challenge,

Don't let me face it lone.

As one we'll meet the shadow.

As one we'll make it home.

They crept closer. I put both hands on my sword. I knew what came next.

For I know that love is with me,

For I know the truth I hold.

A home to hold and keep me.

A love to know my very own.

The watchers froze, and I heard something else. A loud voice bellowed from behind them.

"A love like no other. A love I'll find in you alone."

Two familiar faces emerged from the wood. Both were more worn than I had ever seen them, but I had never felt more warmth for other human beings in my life. Stumbling from the forest, their arms wrapped around each other, were Matthew and Cornelius.

Both were bloody and torn and both had their weapons in their free hands, the ends glowed white. The watchers backed up.

"Matthew! Cornelius!" I shouted.

"Together, brother!" shouted Cornelius.

I turned and faced the watchers.

I heard the priests sing, and I joined in with them as we advanced on the watchers.

"For I know that love is with me! For I know the truth I hold!"

The watchers turned and fled into the forest. I ran to the two men. Reaching them, I threw my arms around them like they were my long-lost father. I pulled them tight, tears sprung to my eyes and laughter to my lips.

"I thought you were both dead. I thought you both were dead, you fools."

"We thought the same," said Matthew, patting me on the pack.

I took a step back. I saw a softness in Cornelius' face that had not been there before.

"How are you, dear friend?" Cornelius reached forward and grabbed my shoulder, smiling.

"Seeing you two, I am well," I said.

We all laughed and embraced again. Then the questions came flooding.

"How?" I asked. "How did you find me?"

Matthew laughed and held up a hand behind me.

"The fire helped."

I turned around and stared at the fire. Its existence had slipped my mind. I shook my head and laughed, smacking my palm against my head.

"Of course."

"Though your awful singing helped," said Cornelius with a smile.

"What…what happened to you?"

The holy men talked to me about how they had landed near one another on the forest floor. The horrors they had faced wandering through. Then they saw the light and followed it.

I told them the story of the mystic. They both said prayers for the poor man. There was a moment of silence after my tale. Then we heard twigs snapping. We spun and more impossible forms walked out of the forest.

But these forms were welcome.

Alexei at the fore, nearly carrying Sacha with one hand. Behind him walked Warin, Hunter, and Fion. I rushed to them and slammed against Fion. We rocked back and forth as we embraced one another.

They had all found me the same way, through the fire. We gathered by it. They told me their stories. They had all fallen near each other and survived by working together. I told them of the mystic and their faces darkened.

The mood soon shifted. We sang songs as the world darkened around us. Arms around one another. For the first time in a long time, we felt warmth, safety, and love.

But there was one thing that bothered me.

I had seen a knight still atop the landing. One that had not fallen with us. And yet the only other two knights were here with me and had both fallen.

I shook my head and lost myself in the singing. Probably a trick of the eye. After all, who can tell what madness exists in this world?

And I know one thing.

Right now, I don't care.

Chapter 27

I stared at the last dying ember of the fire. We had sung and danced through the night, but now there was nothing but a dying flame before us. What we were going to do next pressed on our minds.

I had been so happy to see the others that thoughts of the task before us had drifted from my mind. The relief was nice for a time. But now we stared at the last of our refuge and none of us knew what came next.

Warin stared at the woods, scanning it like one who has been hunted before. None of us came from that wood without experiencing the darkness within. Though I was the only one to lose my companion.

My thoughts drifted to the wet squishing sound his skin made as it slapped against the ground. I shuddered and held myself tighter.

"Alaric."

I looked up. Warin stared at me.

"We found something in our journey, something that we wanted everyone to see."

Dark looks crossed Alexei's and Sacha's faces.

"What did they find?" I asked.

"It's best if we show you."

I sighed and hung my head. The time for reverie was over. I forced myself up and dusted myself off. The rest of the companions had already risen. I looked at Warin.

"Lead the way."

Warin led us back through the wood, down to where the trees pressed tight together and a feeling of being trapped permeated the air. We took twists and turns down a rocky gulley. There, Warin showed us what they had seen.

There was an open wound in the earth, a passage that led into darkness. Red and purple laced the edges, as if the tear was through a living thing. Darkness emanated from the wound.

I cupped a hand to my mouth and looked at Warin.

"Why bring us here?"

Warin sighed. "You know why."

I looked at the wound. At the edge of the darkness, deeper in, I saw a faint light.

"You want us to go down there?"

"It leads somewhere."

"Somewhere we want to go?"

"You feel it." Warin faced me in full. "You feel the power that emanates from it…" Warin looked down; his eyes clouded for a moment. "We're all together again. We need to take advantage of it. See if we can complete this quest or not."

"I'll not go to my death, Alexei." said Sacha. "I won't go."

Alexei set a hand on his brother's shoulder. "You shall not die, Sacha. I shall preserve you."

I looked at the wound.

"Where does it lead?"

"It's not deep," said Warin. "Fion explored it a little before he met up with us. Fion."

We all turned to my friend. Fion stared at the hole, frowning. He gritted his teeth and seemed in pain.

"What lies beyond?" I asked.

Fion looked at me, our eyes meeting. I saw restrained panic on his face.

"More of this cursed world. I didn't venture far. I was scared. A darkness lives there, even more powerful than here."

"Which is why that is where we must go," Cornelius spoke and walked between us. "We must go where things are darkest. Only there can we help spread the light."

Hunter chuckled. The cartographer had said little during our time of peace. The madness that had been there before still seemed to lurk just around the corner.

Everyone else ignored the cartographer.

"Hunter," I said. "Do you know anything about this place?"

Cornelius frowned but said nothing. Hunter shrugged, looking up towards the treetops.

"I know nothing, knight. I am simply here. Awaiting what is coming for us all."

"Death comes regardless of what we do," said Cornelius. "I'd suggest you find something better to worry about. In the meantime, we must move."

Cornelius held up his mace and held an open palm towards the wound. Bright white light emanated from his hand.

"We shall use my light. Now hasten. This takes energy."

Cornelius led the way into the darkened wound. I followed. I stepped through the wound on a squishy, darkened floor. It was not long before we emerged on the other side and had entered a new world.

We stood on a high hill. Stretching before us were rolling hills, castles perched atop the far ones. A great black ocean seethed to the left, a great blackened fort stood near the surf. Off to the left were grassy hills that led to a giant black wall.

There was less fog in this section of the world. It clung to the lower parts, obscured what there was from view.

We ventured into the land. The presence of the land was different. There was a darker energy to it. I heard a great shriek and looked up. In the fog above, I saw a dark shape, or part of it, flit through the clouds.

But it had to be an effect of the weather, for no creature could be so large.

Cornelius discovered a path that meandered down towards ruins, where fog covered parts of the ancient structures. As we descended a cracked set of stairs, the presence grew stronger. We found a broken path at the base of the stairs, leading to a building off to the right.

The building had a great bronze dome that gleamed with the strange green light of the land. Columns went around the building with stairs leading up to the entrance. The interior was dark. The dark presence seemed to emanate from the place.

Cornelius turned at the bottom of the stairs and headed towards the dome. I stopped, my heart quickening. I thought of how alone I had felt, had quick madness came to those without support in this land.

I looked at the dome. I did not know what it contained, but I knew whatever it was would break the party. Even if we overcame whatever was inside, we would not exit the same people we went in as.

"Cornelius," I said.

The confessor turned and stared at me.

"Can we wait?" I asked.

He raised an eyebrow. "Wait? Wait for what?"

"We cannot wait, Alaric," said Warin.

He knew me too well.

"I…I…" I felt foolish.

I looked at the dome.

"Something dwells there. Something dark."

Cornelius nodded. "Which is why we're moving there."

"Are we ready?"

"We will never be ready," replied Cornelius. "But we must go anyway."

Hunter laughed at the back of the group. I turned and saw others give the cartographer darkened looks. Matthew laid a firm hand on Hunter's shoulder.

"Please, Hunter," said Matthew. "Enough of this."

The monk shook. I turned back to Cornelius.

"We…"

Cornelius nodded. He leaned forward and whispered.

"I feel it too. The fear that wants me to turn back, to forget about the task we have before us. But we must set on."

Cornelius leaned back and looked around.

"What other choice do we have?"

I nodded. Warin walked over and gave me a nudge.

"We will prevail. We must."

We resumed our trek to the domed building. All the way, Hunter chuckled in a low voice. We were halfway to the building when Fion whirled on him. I saw madness in my friend's eyes and lunged for him.

Fion's sword was halfway to Hunter when I deflected it with my own.

"Silence him!" shouted Fion, as I crashed against his body and pushed him away.

Warin rushed up and grabbed Fion. We pulled him from the path.

"I would not kill him," said Fion. "Just give him a light wound. Silence his damned mouth. We've been through enough as it is. He's been like this the entire time. Some cartographer, you're nothing but a drain on us all!"

"Peace, Fion." I grabbed my friend so he looked at me. "Peace, brother."

Fion looked at Hunter, then back at me. Hunter laughed. I heard a loud crack, and the laughing stopped. I turned and saw Hunter doubled over. Matthew stepped back, both his fists balled.

"Now this isn't right," said Matthew, pointing a finger at Hunter as if scolding a child. "This isn't right at all."

I glanced around. We were on a low plain with puddles of water dotting it. Far away was a hill that rose, besides that there were no other living things. Feeling safe from the outside, I turned back in.

Hunter stepped away, his eyes roving between us all.

"Don't any of you get it?" he asked. "You're still not getting it. You stupid fools, you still don't get it."

Hunter removed the flask from his side and tried draining some back, but it was gone. He threw the flask to the ground. It clattered against the grass and lay still.

"You're all fools," he said, "a bunch of meddling fools. You don't defeat this land, no one does. Including Aldin and whatever other fools have ventured here."

"I'll have his head." Fion walked between me and Warin.

We both lunged forward and yanked him back.

"Take my head." Hunter's voice was loud and shrill. "Take it. What does it matter? There are far worse deaths than a swing of the sword."

Hunter looked at the dome.

"I'm...I'm going to deliver us all. You wait and see." He laughed and sprinted towards the dome.

"Stop him," said Cornelius.

"Darkness! Demons! Devils! All sorts of nasty lot!" Hunter screamed at the top of his lungs as he tore off for the dome.

The mad cartographer was fast. Not weighed down by equipment or weapon, he was much faster than us.

"We need to stop him!" shouted Cornelius.

Cornelius, Matthew, and Sacha lined up. They prepared spells. I watched as Hunter moved closer to the dome.

"Wake up! Wake up! The day is here and there are lives to take!" Shouted the cartographer. "Come one, come all! Come to the feast of souls." Hunter clapped his hands over his head as he ran.

If he hadn't been running towards our doom, I might have been impressed with his coordination and speed.

A white bolt flared in Cornelius' hand. He reared back.

"Wait," said Matthew.

Matthew nudged Cornelius as he threw the bolt making it miss. Cornelius whirled on Matthew, he looked ready to kill the priest.

"Stun him." Matthew's spell was half prepared and of a different sort than Cornelius'.

"There's no time." Cornelius turned towards Hunter.

He was a good ways off now, halfway between the stairs that led to the dome and our position. His voice rang out clear over the desolate expanse. Blue light flashed through the air. It screeched towards Hunter and slammed into him.

The cartographer's voice cut off as he smacked to the ground, landing like a sack of coal. I looked over and saw Sacha with his wand extended. A tear slipped from his left eye and he wheezed. He sagged into himself and toppled forward. Matthew ran forward and caught him, holding him up.

"Good work, Sacha," said Cornelius. "You may have just saved the party."

I walked over towards the commotion. Hunter was not moving. I walked over to where Matthew had Sacha propped. Alexei rushed to his brother's side and took him.

"It's alright brother," said Alexei. "You did what you had to."

"You did good." Cornelius walked over and stood in front of Sacha. "Without the element of surprise, there are few things we can best in this land. Though even that may be gone now."

"I didn't want to kill him," said Sacha. "I didn't want to do that. You know that, Alexei. It's not my intention to kill, not humans. I'm not like you. I've never done that before. I'm scared."

Sacha buckled forward and hurled. I turned away, set a hand to my mouth, heard the wet splash against the ground.

"There, there." Alexei's voice was tender. "There, there, sweet brother. You did what you must."

"You're a hero, Sacha," said Cornelius. "You saved the party."

"I don't feel like it," said Sacha, spit dripped from his lips.

I felt bad for the boy. He was clearly unused to fighting, and it was a wonder what sent him on this venture. I looked over at Warin. Warin looked concerned. He saw me looking and sighed.

"Sacha." He walked over and knelt in front of Sacha. "It's never easy the first time."

"I don't want it to ever be easy," replied Sacha.

Warin nodded. "And I cannot blame you for that. But you did what was required, what we needed."

Sacha nodded. I looked at Hunter. A wisp of smoke rose from his back. A few minutes later, we moved towards the dome again. We passed Hunter and Sacha looked away. I glanced down and saw a smoldering hole through Hunter's back.

His head tilted to the side, and one of his arms had tangled up under him. His eyes were open, and he stared out at the land. I sighed and looked forward.

He was gone and our destiny lay ahead.

Chapter 28

We walked up the steps leading into the domed building. It vibrated with dark energy. I heard a low hum emanate from the dome, almost as if a quiet church service was going on.

I was first to reach the top of the stairs. The building had a layer of pillars that went around the dome. Further in was a wall inlaid with a mosaic of heroes battling strange and horrifying creatures. The mosaic stretched around the entire building, or at least the parts I could see.

Directly before us were two large open brass doors. Inside was darkness. I could hear my heart hammering in my ears. Cornelius walked ahead of me. He paused at the doors. The low hum was louder now.

He looked at us. We gathered round. He leaned forward and cleared his throat. He whispered.

"I do not know what we will see beyond these doors. I do not know what demon we shall encounter. But I know it will not be pleasant." His eyes roamed from companion to companion. "What lies ahead will try us, of that, I am sure."

He cleared his throat again.

"We will overcome, we will prevail, for the Light is with us. Once more, we will witness homes free from danger. We will have a peaceful kingdom once again. I know this, I see this. And we shall do all in our power to ensure that this comes about…and I know I am not the only one that shares this belief."

He looked to Warin.

"Any words, Master Knight?"

"You speak true," said Warin. "We shall go, and we shall prevail."

Cornelius nodded.

"Then let it be done"

Cornelius turned and was the first to enter the darkness. Warin went after. I was third. As I pushed through the door, it felt like the darkness clung to me like a sheet. I kept on. The blackness pressed against me as if it tried to keep me out.

It got to where I felt like I was underwater and the cloying darkness pressed against my nose and mouth, threatening to cut off my breathing. Then, as soon as I felt like I was going to struggle for breath, the darkness ended.

I stepped out onto a stone stair, my footstep echoed across the enclosed dome. My eyes adjusted. I saw Cornelius a few stairs down from me and Warin the next stair down. They were both staring at what lay at the center of the dome.

The dome had stairs that went down towards the middle, where there was a landing. On that landing was a beast of strange proportion. It squatted on a throne far too small for it. Its hooved feet perched on the black throne.

Its back was to us, but it had two pairs of folded black wings. I saw two long arms that ended in claws. The claws drug along the ground on either side of the throne. The creature's head bowed forward, but I could discern four horns protruding from the back of its hairy mane.

I heard others emerge from the blackness and make loud steps onto the stairs. I whirled. Fion came through and I grabbed him before he could step.

"It doesn't matter," said Cornelius. "That thing knows we are here."

As if on cue, the creature stood on the throne and rose to its full height, which was three times our own. It expanded its wings then turned to us. Its ribs pressed against its sickly yellow skin, looking like they'd tear through. The creature wore a black, tattered cloth around its waist. I looked up at its face and shuddered. The remains of a black hood hung down over the skull of an ox.

The creature turned to us. Mixed with the presence of darkness was the stench of animal decay. The creature let out a bleating cry and stumbled towards us. It took its first step and collapsed against the stairs.

It looked up at us and reached out a shaking hand. Its claws clacked along the stairs. It let out another long bleat that sounded like the cry of an elk. Its claws dug into the stairs, cracking the stone. It tried pulling itself towards us.

I saw matted red fur along its stomach and legs, as if someone had wounded the creature.

"What darkness," gasped Cornelius.

The confessor already prepared a spell. I looked down at the hobbling creature. As horrifying as it was, it seemed pathetic. It let out another long bleat that sent a chill down my spine.

I walked towards the creature.

"Let's be done with it," I said. "Put the brute out of its misery."

We spread out and approached the creature. It wheezed as it tried to move. I heard Cornelius muttering words in an ancient language. Then a white flash of light cut across my vision. The creature raised its forearm, and the white arc slammed against it.

I smelled burning flesh and heard the sizzle and pop of the creature's decayed skin. It let another mournful wail. Then a change went through the creature. Something vibrated along its body. Its head snapped forward, and it pushed itself up with its forearms.

It balanced itself on its wobbly legs and leaned back, letting out a wailing screech that had us all ducking and covering our ears.

The creature advanced. It towered above us like a tree from a nightmare.

It moved towards Cornelius. Warin and Fion rushed for its leg. The creature looked down and swung at them. My heart leapt into my throat as its claws brushed by Warin, nearly taking out my commander.

I ran towards the monster. Alexei leapt in front of Cornelius, brandishing his sword. The creature let out another bellow and swept Alexei away. Alexei crashed against the stone and went rolling down.

I feared we had lost another.

Sacha stepped forward and a bright blue flash shot from his wand. The blue streak slammed against the creature's face. The creature turned away, moaning. Warin reached its legs. He leapt in and swung with all his might. His sword sliced through the creature's ankle and lodged itself halfway in.

Warin released his sword and rolled away as the creature's claws pulverized where he had stood a moment before. Fion was next to enter, thrusting his sword into the creature's wounded thigh. The blade sank in, and the creature screeched.

Fion released his sword and ducked away as the monster's claws almost took him. A bolt of light from Cornelius slammed into the monster's chest, knocking it back a few paces.

I was next to close in. I looked down at its sword free ankle. With a well-placed blow, I could sever it. I leapt and swung; my blade got stuck halfway through. I knew better than to retrieve it, so I leapt for the stairs.

Flecks of stone hit me as the creature destroyed where I had just stood. I hit the stairs and rolled down; the wind knocked out of me. I looked up and saw the creature kick out then swipe at Warin. It connected. Warin twisted and crashed down the stairs.

I felt sick. Warin slumped against the stairs and did not move. The creature leapt up the stairs, its ankles gave out as it did. It raked out with its claws, Matthew, Sacha, and Cornelius all went to the ground.

The creature's ankles split, spilling black ichor onto the stairs. I was on my feet and rushed towards the beast. The creature clawed its way forward, outdistancing me. I saw Sacha up against the walls of the building.

Tears rolled down his eyes as he held his feeble wand out towards the beast. The creature reared back and swung. I saw Matthew. Where he came from, I don't know. He stood before the beast and held his hands out.

A shield of gold energy shot around him and Sacha. The creature's claws slammed against the energy. I heard a great cry, and the claws rebounded off, burned. The shield shattered and Matthew fell to the ground.

Sacha stood, and another blue beam of light snaked into the creature's neck. I saw Alexei's sword and snatched it up. The creature used its one good hand to swipe at Sacha.

Sacha raced away. The creature followed Sacha's movement and went to intercept him. But I was there. I drove Alexei's sword deep underneath the fallen creature's chin up through its skull, where it emerged on the other side, black ichor spilled off it.

The creature shuddered and slumped. I could not take the weight of its head and released the sword. As the head collided with the stone, I instinctively took a step back. I fell, panting. I watched the creature, expecting it to come roaring to life.

A felt pressure on my shoulder that made me spin.

"Peace."

It was Cornelius. He panted, and blood covered his face. His robe had great gashes along the front soaked with blood.

"Are…are you alright?" I asked.

He nodded.

"Yes…I think so. Sacha."

Cornelius looked over. Sacha walked towards him. He was bloody as well.

"Matthew…," said Sacha.

I looked to where Matthew had been. I stood up as Sacha raced by me. He flitted around the creature and fell to his knees on the other side.

"No!" wailed Sacha.

I leapt up and raced over. Matthew lay sprawled out on the ground. The man's arms looked pulverized, as if a heavy stone had rolled over them. Blood leaked from his shoulders. He had a glazed look in his eyes. Sacha cradled him like a baby.

"Matthew," said Sacha.

I looked down and saw Alexei walking up the stairs, a hand to his head. Further down, Fion helped Warin limp up.

We lost less than I thought. I looked down at Matthew. He coughed and blood sputtered from his mouth.

"This is my fault. This is my fault," said Sacha.

"No, it is not," said Cornelius.

"Sacha." Matthew spoke through bloodied teeth, his words labored.

"Sacha, it is not your fault, my boy. I did what I had to."

I could only imagine the pain Matthew was in.

"And I would gladly do it again," said Matthew, the strength returned to his voice for a moment.

Sacha cried.

Cornelius knelt by Matthew. "My skills are far less than yours, brother, but I shall try."

Cornelius rubbed his hands together, and they glowed white.

"Save your strength, friend," said Matthew. "You'll need it on the road ahead."

Cornelius set his glowing palms against Matthew's shoulders. White light pulsed into them.

"You are kind, friend," said Matthew. "But my time is at an end."

"Not yet," replied Cornelius.

The confessor's face shone red. Sweat poured off him, mixing with the blood and dripped onto the floor.

"The light that does not fade has come for me at last," said Matthew. "How beautiful it is. Live well brothers, for I shall see you all again soon."

Cornelius applied more healing to Matthew, but the monk leaned back, and his eyes went blank. Cornelius fell against him, as did Sacha.

I looked up at Warin. His face was grim, and his eyes set. Blood covered his armor, as well as Fion's. Alexei stood on wobbly legs; he looked down at Matthew as if he was unsure what he looked at.

This world took more from us than we could bear.

We would not last much longer.

Chapter 29

I walked out and looked up at the sky. The cracks still shone bright. I collapsed against the stairs. I felt hands on me, pushing me up.

"Get up," said Warin, "up, none of that."

I looked at the others. Sacha's face was numb, far from the curious lad that started the journey with us. Cornelius held his hand close to his stomach. Alexei seemed unharmed aside from being a little dazed. Fion had a wrap around his neck stained with blood. Warin had a wrap around his face, covering a chunk of missing skin.

Cornelius walked out onto the waste.

"We must press forward."

None of us questioned it. None of us fought. We plodded forward. Across the desolate wastes, we traveled, entering a land of undulating hills.

I looked up at the confessor. Something pressed him on, something I envied, something I feared. Warin walked next to him. I knew the old warrior's discipline was deep, but I did not think this deep.

Periodically he looked back at us, studying us, making sure we were okay I guessed. Though it never could be. We wandered through the hills and entered a fog drenched path.

In the distance, we heard the thunder of some horrible beast. But instead of fear, I felt less and less. Death seemed like a better option than pressing on. The finality of it brought a comfort that preserving did not have.

A white light shone ahead, dissipating the nearby fog. Cornelius guided us through. We emerged from the fog bank and stared out over more hills, but something was different. Here, dotting the hills, were palaces and castles of gold, though the gold was old and tarnished. Vines grew up the sides of the palaces, and mist seeped in and out of their openings. I spotted a stained-glass window that someone had shattered some time ago.

Cornelius looked over at the vista and sighed. He turned to Warin.

"What do you think, Master Knight?" asked Cornelius. "Is this the way forward?"

Warin studied the land.

"I don't know, confessor. All paths seem equal right now."

Cornelius nodded. "I felt a call here, so I heeded it."

"Then let's see what we find," replied Warin.

I did not feel like talking. I barely felt like existing. My only way out was death from the waking nightmare that trapped me. The numbness I felt surprised me. I heard sniffing and turned. Sacha shivered and Alexei held a hand on his back.

"Peace, brother," said Alexei. "We will prevail."

"He died on my behalf," replied Sacha, his voice a wisp.

"Brother…" Alexei seemed to struggle to find words. "Brother, he did what he must. No different from you or I."

"I wish it were me," replied Sacha.

"Shh, shh." Alexei pulled his brother close, rocking him. "Do not speak such foolishness."

A few moments later, we headed down to the golden land before us. Cornelius found a path that cut along one hill and emerged at the base of the nearest palace. I looked up at a great crystalline dome sitting atop the front of the golden palace. The rest of the palace was higher on the hill and lost to view.

Cornelius stood at the entrance to the palace, staring down its darkened hall. I felt no darkness, no presence emanated from it. The land was dead. Both darkness and light had long ago deserted it.

"What are we searching for?" I asked.

"We don't know," replied Warin.

"What about a way home?" I asked.

Everyone in the group turned to me.

"A way home for what?" asked Warin.

"A way home…" I glanced around, hoping to see support in the staring faces. "We've pushed ourselves to the limit. We can go home, we've done our part. Others can come."

"Alaric." Cornelius spoke.

He caught me off guard. I was not sure he remembered my name.

"Yes, Cornelius?" I asked.

He held out his hands to the surrounding land.

"Go home to what?"

"What do you mean?" I asked. "Go home to family, to be with loved ones while we can."

"What you see here," said Cornelius. "Is coming to our home."

"And we can't stop it," I replied. "We've lost three people, and the cracks have barely changed. What more can we do? If we go home, at least we can spend time with those we love before the rest of the horrors come through."

"Alaric," said Warin. "Perish the thought."

I shook my head.

"I want to see them again before I die."

Warin nodded.

"I know. We all want to see those we love."

The numbness gave way to panic. The reality of what happened pressed in on me, threatened to overcome my mind.

"Be strong, Alaric," said Alexei. "We will see the day. We will prevail."

I looked at Alexei. He seemed sure of himself. The light in his eyes had not faded as much as I had thought.

"I…"

Warin stepped forward and placed a hand on my shoulder.

"We are here for you, Alaric. As you have been for us."

"That we are," echoed Cornelius.

I sighed.

"You do not want this to come to them. Sure, we may have a few more hours with our loved ones, but they will suffer horrible deaths if this world comes through. Right now, we have a chance, even if slim, to prevent that."

"I realize that, Warin," I said. "But the chances…"

"Are slim, I know. We all know."

I looked at Fion. He said nothing. He stared into the palace, but I knew he felt the same as me. I shook my head.

"Forget I said anything."

"It's okay, Alaric." said Warin. "We all have our troubles, our doubts."

"Best not to take heed of them," said Cornelius. "Not if you want to make a difference here."

"Let's keep moving," said Sacha. "I don't like standing still here."

So we entered the darkened palace.

We walked down great halls made for giants. We entered a grand cathedral room with jewels and glass sparkling off the dim light from cracks in the ceiling.

We walked down a dusty hall and into an ancient throne room.

And it was there that we met the old, ruined king.

Chapter 30

An old man stood before us. It was clear he had been a warrior in his youth. Even with his bent frame, he still stood near my height. He wore a heavy fur cloak that swallowed him. An ancient crown of gold was atop his head. He had sunken eyes and leaned against an iron rod. He stared at us, puffing as if exhausted.

"Sir," said Warin. "Greetings. We are strangers to this land. What is your name?"

The man's eyes flashed to Warin, intensity shone deep in them.

"I am King Arcanus. Ruler of these lands, or I was…"

Arcanus adjusted his staff, wincing whenever he had to shift his weight.

"What are you doing in my land?"

"We are adventurers from another realm."

"Another realm?" The old king raised a bushy eyebrow. "What other realm?"

Warin looked at Cornelius.

"Do you know what happened to your kingdom?" asked Cornelius.

The confessor walked forward and bowed before the king.

"We rid your land of demons."

"Demons?" asked the king. "In my land? I'd never stand for it. Surely this is some sort of misunderstanding."

"You're to tell me this land is free of demons, my king?" asked Cornelius.

"Of course." Arcanus' voice boomed through the hall.

"There are others here?" asked Warin.

"Others?" asked Arcanus.

"Subjects," said Cornelius.

The old king nodded. "Of course, thousands. Come, I'll show you."

The old king turned around and shuffled down the hall. We followed him towards a large iron door. The door was ajar. The king slipped in and motioned us forward. I walked in and stopped.

Ahead of me was a room with four pillars holding the roof. The open spaces between the pillars looked out over the valley below. Even in the decay, it was a beautiful sight. I walked out towards the center of the room and felt a breeze.

Old tapestries hung from the ceiling and fluttered. On them I saw pictures of many people, all in gold. Arcanus walked towards the ledge overlooking the land below. He stopped a foot from it and stared.

When we were all in the room, Arcanus spun on his heels and bowed.

"Gentlemen. You have journeyed far. Please allow me to introduce you to my lovely Queen Rikke."

Arcanus shuffled over to a chair with a cover over it. He grabbed the cover and pulled it free. There, on the throne, was the decayed body of a woman. Her thinned hair clung to her browned skin.

Her eyes were closed, her skin cracked and stretched like leather. She wore a white dress that was torn in places.

"Rikke, these are our guests," said Arcanus.

He sat, stared at her, waiting. I looked to Warin. He was unnerved.

We should have known better than to think the first person we encounter in this land would be sane.

"She's not talkative right now," said Arcanus.

He laughed and shook his head.

"Forgive me, my guests." he turned away from her and puttered back to his spot overlooking the valley.

He breathed in deep and sighed.

"Isn't it lovely?" he asked.

I walked over and looked down into the valley. I caught demons stalking through the land here and there.

"What happened here?" asked Sacha.

Arcanus glanced over his shoulder, his face twisted for a moment.

"What does he mean?" asked the king. His voice was so low I could barely hear him.

I thought the question was for me, but something told me he asked himself.

"What is he talking about?" asked Arcanus, staring at the mist below.

"King, sire," said Cornelius, walking over and standing next to Arcanus.

"We came to hunt demons. You wouldn't know their whereabouts, would you? We need a place to look."

Arcanus smiled and waved Cornelius off.

"You church lot are always so funny. There's no demon in our land, Jaxus, so stop asking the question. There're no demons here, confessor, just men. But maybe that's enough? Is it not?"

"Not right now," replied Cornelius, stepping away.

"Where are the people?" asked Warin.

"The queen won't convince you of this land's prosperity, but the people will." Arcanus laughed and walked away from the ledge.

"I'll show you where the lesser live."

He walked us out to another part of the palace. We walked out onto a long walkway that overlooked a grotto below.

Dead bodies piled on each other; evidence of struggle clear. Some were naked, many had their legs tucked up and their hands covered as they huddled on the floor of the grotto.

"The people slumber," said Arcanus. "They're waiting. Soon we'll venture from this place. Ever since the fog came…"

"The fog?" asked Cornelius. "You see, the fog?"

Arcanus turned to us, his eyes were different.

"What do you mean?"

"What happened?" I stepped forward, locked eyes with Arcanus. "What happened here?"

Arcanus shrugged. "We learned to live with them."

"Who?"

"Those that came."

"The demons?"

Arcanus stared at the floor and did not answer.

"They were friendly at first, but then they brought the others…why…why are those people sleeping? What are they doing?"

Arcanus walked to the precipice and looked over his people.

"Oh…oh this isn't good. They're…what happened here? I…I must talk to Rikke. Let her know. We must call Reinhard. He is my son. He will bring the knights. We will rally. We will beat this. You…"

Arcanus pointed at me.

"Come, Knight. We must wage war. We must save them. This is a travesty. Come, we will make war, and we will…"

Arcanus stopped.

"I…" the fire had left his eyes.

He blinked a few times and looked around.

"Why are you all here?"

Cornelius sighed and wiped his face. Warin walked over and placed a hand on the king's shoulder.

"We didn't fight them when they came and then it was too late…" said Arcanus.

"What?" I asked.

But the king was gone again. The husk returned. The king wobbled forward.

"I have to find…something…what all, what all did you want again?"

I looked at the bodies below. Mothers cradled their children. Men huddled together, back-to-back. Fathers with their arms around their families. Hundreds of them, stretching as far as I could see.

That was the fate of all who were in this land.

That was the fate that awaited my family.

This land was once greater than our own, and it fell.

I clutched my chest.

Was there no escape from this madness?

Chapter 31

We sat in the king's throne room. He leaned towards the decayed husk of his wife, running a hand along her chin.

"My lovely, Rikke."

The king let out a contented sigh and sat back, staring at us. We sat around the king, shifting uncomfortably. Death covered the surrounding land. I sat, my hands folded in front of me, alternating between despair and anger.

"Dear king," said Warin, "we want to know where the great demons lie. Where we can seek them out to destroy them."

The king's face darkened.

"There are no demons in my land," said Arcanus. "I keep the demons away from my land. Why do…why do you all keep saying there are demons? They are not demons, misunderstood maybe, but not demons."

Arcanus studied the ground in front of him, his breath came faster and faster.

"They're not demons. I'd never let demons in. No…no the people, they're the demons. They're the actual demons…"

"The people are dead," I said.

Arcanus shook his head and shut his eyes.

"No, no. That's wrong, they're alive."

"We are wasting our time here," said Alexei. "We should move and find greater demons."

"Maybe he is a demon," said Cornelius, frowning.

Warin held up a hand.

"Dear king. Look around you. Tell me what you see."

The king looked up; his eyes wide as he looked at the room.

"I'm in my throne room. My wife is by my side. My knights are out on errands across the kingdom. All is well."

Alexei sighed. "Come, no good wasting our time here."

"I agree with Alexei," said Cornelius.

"There is but one blight," said the king.

"One blight?" I asked.

The king nodded. "But one blight."

"Where?" asked Warin.

"The castle…on the hillside." Arcanus shook his head. "Such a dark place. He lives there…none of my knights can prosper while he lives."

"Who is he?" I asked.

"The fallen knight," replied Arcanus.

I looked over at Warin.

"Sounds like where we should go."

Warin nodded.

"What is the way there?" I asked.

"No, no, no." The king stood and paced around the room. "You'll not go there. You'll stay here and enjoy merriment with me. It's been so long since I've had guests."

Arcanus cleared his throat.

"I'll summon the page."

Arcanus clapped his hands.

"Reginald. Reginald, come here. We have guests to entertain."

Arcanus stood, tapped his foot, stared at an empty doorway.

"Where is that boy?" he asked.

"There is no boy," I said.

Frustration shot up my spine. I stood up.

"Your people are dead and gone."

The king ignored me. I walked towards him.

"They're dead and gone and ours will be next if we do not do something. Tell us, King Arcanus, how do we get to this castle?"

"We don't even know if the castle has demons," said Sacha.

"They cover this land," said Cornelius. "No doubt we will find what we seek there."

"The people are fine," said Arcanus.

I stepped forward and grabbed the king by his coat, turning him to face me.

"Alaric," said Warin.

"Time is slipping away for us. Tell us where to go and we will be on our way."

"Enjoy it here." Replied the king, his eyes glazed.

I shook him.

"Where is this castle?" I asked. "Tell us where. Now."

"Alaric."

A few voices called my name behind me. I ignored them and shook the king harder.

"Where is it? Your people are all dead you fool, you're living in a delusion. Where is it? Where is the damn castle? Tell me!"

My voice rose with every syllable. I screamed in the king's face as he stared blankly at me.

"Dammit." I pounded one fist against the king's chest. "Dammit, they could already be through by now. We don't have time. Dammit, why won't you just tell me?"

I released the king, and he fell a few steps back. I felt hands on me, pulling me away.

"We don't have time. I don't want the demons to get them next. I can't have that happen. Speak now Arcanus or I'll run you through myself."

My friends restrained me.

Arcanus took a few halting steps towards me. There was intelligence in his eyes that had not been there a moment before.

"I…"

The intelligence faded.

"We must have a feast. I'll call Reginald."

"No!"

I shot forward, my sword drawn. I knocked the king to his knees and held my sword to his chin.

"Tell me where this castle is now. Tell me and I may go."

"Why are you doing this? I'll call my knights. Reginald! Reginald."

I took a step back and let my sword clatter to the floor. I fell to my knees and wrapped my hands around myself.

"I don't want to lose them," I said. "We don't have time. I don't want to lose them."

I felt weak, I felt small, I felt sick.

I felt many things at that moment, none of them good. I felt a hand on my shoulder.

"Alaric," said Fion. "It's alright brother."

"But it's not, Fion," I replied.

"I know," said Fion.

Fion squatted next to me.

"But this won't change it."

I looked up and saw the king stared at me. There was a glint of personality in his eyes.

"I can't allow what happened here to happen to them," I said.

The king continued to stare.

"I'll do anything…anything to see that they are safe." I looked at Fion. "You know that."

Fion nodded. "That I do."

I looked back at the king.

"The castle," said the king. "I'll show you the gate."

Chapter 32

Arcanus had not lied.

A dark cloud hung over the land ahead of us. A rickety path led over a deep chasm towards a black castle perched high on a hillside. Fog billowed all around the land where the castle perched.

It wafted up over the jagged path, obscuring parts of it from view.

Alexei stood at the front of the path and sighed.

"I feel like a hero of old," he said, staring up at the castle.

He puffed up his chest. Out of all of us, he seemed the least affected by this cursed land. Sacha stood by his side, looking pensive. He clung close to his brother.

"I fear what lies inside," said Sacha.

"As any sane person would," said Cornelius. "Still, that is where we must go. May the Higher One preserve us."

I stood at the start of the path. It resembled a bolt of lightning leading up to the yawning gates of the castle. A steep drop on either side.

I set one foot on the path. A power resonated through the path like a musical hum in the air. It chilled me. I looked up at the castle.

If there was anywhere that would change the cracks, that would lead to us going home, this was it. I realized I shivered as I set another foot on the path. Whatever lay in the castle above was a far greater power than anything we had yet faced.

The wrongness of what lay there weighed heavy on me. I took another step on the path. The drop off on either side gave me less fear than the castle ahead. Gulping, I took a few more halting steps onto the path.

I heard others behind me. Alexei stepped around me and took the lead. I stiffened as he passed. There was scant room to pass each other on the path.

His golden armor twinkled in the twilight. I followed him up the path. We all held hands on the parts lost in the fog. Alexei pushed out his foot here and there to find what was open space and what was solid ground.

Together, as a team, as a brotherhood. We made our way to the gates of the castle. The fog clung to the floor of the castle and the inside was devoid of all light.

Cornelius stepped to the fore. He held his hand out and a white light shone ahead of us.

"I'll lead the way."

We stepped into the castle, and all stopped.

The air in the castle was thick, it smelled of sulfur and death. Sacha restrained a cough.

"We'll take a second to adjust," said Cornelius. "Then we shall continue our quest."

My eyes stung, I wiped them. Combined with the smells was a thickness to the air, a presence weighed on us. It was like what I had felt at the dragon shrine.

But here, the presence was different. It was not as strong as the shrine had been, but there was a distinct quality to it. While the power of the shrine folded over you like a wet blanket, this power struck at my mind, as if trying to pierce it.

"I don't like it here," said Sacha.

"Peace, brother," said Alexei. "We shall prevail."

"Let us move," said Cornelius.

It was clear the atmosphere would not improve. As we ventured further into the castle hall, it only got worse. Cornelius led us to a set of wide stairs that led to a large arched opening. The blackness pulsed from beyond the arch.

I tasted spoiled meat. I wanted to spit, but the chamber was so quiet I didn't dare disturb it. The pressure in my mind was like a dagger that pried at my skull.

The presence no longer felt like part of the environment, but a living thing. Something tried to get into my mind, to get at my heart. I saw a flash of light as Cornelius' hand glowed brighter.

The dagger in my mind turned back to a dull thud.

"We should not be without a strong light in this place," said Cornelius.

Cornelius led us forward through the arch. The blackness seemed to lighten, and a low light illuminated parts of the room. I could tell we were in a cathedral of sorts. We could see broken pews pressed against the walls to our left and right, ragged and torn tapestries hung from the wall. Ahead of us was a small set of stairs that led to a raised platform with an altar.

It was from the altar I felt the presence.

I heard Cornelius gasp. "This was a church, and a grand one of that."

Cornelius wandered from the straight path and examined the altar.

"What is this?" hissed Cornelius. "This was a holy place."

There was anger in Cornelius' voice.

"What is this?" His voice was louder, echoing through the room.

"Cornelius," whispered Fion. "Keep your voice down. We don't know what lies in this place."

Cornelius kicked a bit of the rubble, sent it skirting across the floor.

"I want to know," he said. "I want to know what lives here, what did this to a holy place."

Cornelius whirled and looked beyond the altar. He turned his light, and we all saw a mark on the wall. It was black with dried blood and was in a blasphemous shape. I did not know the meaning of the symbol, but it filled me with nausea.

"Bastard…" said Cornelius. "That bastard. They'll burn for this…all of them."

"What is it?" asked Warin.

"Darkness, the darkness. It's making a mockery of Him."

Cornelius turned towards us. His eyes blazed with a fierce light.

"When I find the demon that desecrated this holy place, this beautiful place. I shall burn him to ash."

There was a pulse in the air. Something stirred. We all noticed it. Without realizing it, we all pressed together and faced out, our backs pressed against one another. I studied the room, expecting demons to come pouring out from some darkened corner at any moment.

But nothing came.

We waited and waited. Our swords were ready, but nothing came from the darkness. After a few minutes had passed, I lowered my sword. The presence was still strong, but nothing stirred.

"Stay on guard," said Warin. "Something is wrong here."

I couldn't breathe. I reached up and clamped my hand to my throat. A burning sensation crowded out my breath. I coughed and hacked. I teared up, my eyes stinging.

And I felt stark fear.

I looked up through bleary eyes and saw something coming through the arched entrance. Something filled it, a black cloud. Something akin to a strong wind buffeted me back and forth.

But this was no wind. This was something living and something dark. I felt the knives at my skull. They pierced through and entered. Strange thoughts filled my vision. I thought of killing Warin, or throwing Josephine to a pack of hungry demons, of sacrificing Erwin to a strange and dark god.

More dark thoughts crowded in. I felt like I did these things, my hands guided by some force outside of me. The pressure was overwhelming. I was knocked back and forth, the power of the presence too great.

I could not tell if I stood or sat, knelt or was suspended in the air. All I knew was I was not in control and my mind was succumbing to whatever this thing was.

More dark thoughts entered my head. Worse and worse things. At first, I had reacted with horror, but now it seemed the disgusting actions were becoming part of me, were etching themselves in my mind.

My heart twisted beneath the strength of the presence. I tried fighting, but there was nothing to fight, just a blanket of darkness. It threw out my hands but felt nothing.

Darkness swirled around me. I had trouble breathing. Then I saw a flash of light. I oriented myself towards the light. Two more flashes of light. It looked like two eyes and a shouting mouth. Two more flashes that could be hands and then a great flash in the middle. I saw six balls of light swirl in the darkness. It looked like Cornelius, his hands, his eyes, his mouth, and his heart. Another ball of light flared from his solar plexus.

I heard Cornelius' scream reach me in the darkness. It was as if he was burning alive. The light grew, I felt heat from it. Then there was a great flash, an eruption. Something knocked me back.

A scream echoed all around me, then faded into silence. I blinked a few times and realized I stared at the top of the cathedral. I coughed and sat up. Dark sand covered me. I looked around. I saw Fion, and Warin.

Then I saw the mace. Next to it was the charred remains of a skeleton, the bones still glowing with heat.

"Cornelius…" I said.

Warin glanced over and saw the confessor's fate.

"Cornelius," said Warin.

We shuffled over and knelt before the bones. Parts of his robe had somehow survived the blast and stuck to his bones. Everything else was gone, burned away in a holy flame.

I glanced around the room. The suffocating presence was gone. But so were Alexei and Sacha.

I stood up, looking around.

"Where are the brothers?" I asked.

"Cornelius…" repeated Warin.

I looked at the confessor's bones. I shook my head.

"Dammit," I said.

"He gave us a chance," said Fion. "Let's not put it to waste. We need to flee before this place claims who's left."

"I agree." I stared at the bones. I couldn't believe a man had been there a few moments before.

"Thank you, confessor," I said.

"Thank you," echoed Fion.

"Too much sacrifice," I said. "If we stay here, we'll only perish. We can't let their sacrifices die on the vine. Come, we must move."

We both turned to the arched door.

Standing at the door was a wretched creature. A man, perhaps even a knight, seemed to have once inhabited its form. It hunched over. Its back covered in armor. It had two long arms, one held a sword. Its helm, although twisted and torn, still bore the resemblance of a face.

The creature stood the size of two bulls and stared at us. Black ichor leaked off the creature and I knew it was the one that had sent the mist.

It was wounded, but not dead.

I feared what it would take before we slew it.

Chapter 33

The creature moved towards us, ichor spilled from its heart and gut. As it moved, the creature moaned with muted sounds, as if someone had sewn its lips together. It teetered back and forth as it neared us.

"Let's finish it," said Warin.

We spread out to the sides, all approaching from a different angle. The creature reared back on its legs, supporting itself standing for a few moments. Its head whipped back and forth, taking us in. It fell back to its forearms then charged.

The creature moved faster than something so large should be able to move. It bore down on me and swung. I rolled as the blade sliced over me. I came to my feet and was next to the creature.

I searched along its armor for somewhere to pierce but saw nothing. The creature whirled and swung again. I hit the floor; the blade almost nicked my shoulder. Warin and Fion were on the other side of it. Fion struck, and I heard a blade strike metal.

The creature swung out with its forearm and caught Fion in the chest. He rolled across the ground. Warin hacked at the creature's neck. His sword struck the creature's armor, and it buckled under the impact of the blow.

It crawled back, keeping us both in front of it, moaning the entire time. Upon reaching a corner, it reared back onto its feet. It used the wall as support and stayed upright, watching us.

Fion was up and walked with us to corner the monster. The black ichor continued to leak from between the cracks in its armor. A gush of black liquid sprayed from around the creature's knee.

"Where the ichor leaks," I said. "Use your swords there."

The creature fell to the fore and charged again. This time it went after Warin. The creature feinted a blow. Warin rolled, but the creature never attacked. Warin came up from his roll and the creature struck.

Warin leapt back and the tip of the creature's sword caught his stomach and sent him spiraling around. I charged at the creature. On its side, I noticed a spot where the black color seemed to flow. I brought my sword around and dug in.

The creature bucked under the assault. The creature leapt away, tearing my sword from my hands. It crashed against the pews, crushing a few and scattering others. The creature reared up and let out a long moan, like it was trying to scream.

My sword was trapped underneath the creature. Its head swiveled to me, and it charged. I rolled as the monster thundered over me. I stood, and the creature knocked me to the ground. When I looked up, I saw the creature's sword come for me.

Warin leapt in front of me and brought his sword up and into the creature's chest. I cursed the old man. He took too many chances. The creature fell back, Warin's sword stuck into its chest.

Warin yanked the sword free and swung again, slicing into the creature's neck. Ichor started spraying, the creature wobbled back and forth. Warin leapt back as the creature fell to the ground. It moaned and convulsed for a few moments, then lay still.

Warin sank to a knee. I leapt up and rushed over to his side. I grabbed his shoulder as I slid to my knees next to him.

"You saved my life again."

I laughed, trying to wear off the shock of what had just happened. Fion walked over to the creature and sent his sword underneath its chin, ensuring it was dead.

I shook my head.

"The things we have survived in this land," I chuckled. "Thank you." I clapped Warin's shoulder.

I looked over at him.

And realized something was wrong.

He stared at the ground, his face twisted in pain. He clamped a hand to his stomach.

"What is it?" I asked.

"The blow," said Warin. "Please take me to the side."

I looked up at Fion. He looked worried.

"Come."

I grabbed one side of Warin and Fion the other. We took him to the altar and let him lie against it. He coughed, and blood trickled down his lips.

Me and Fion looked at each other.

"Warin," I said. "What happened?"

"The blow," he said.

He removed his hand. The blow had dented his armor into his body. Blood leaked through a puncture.

"Dammit." I leaned my head against the altar.

Warin coughed and more blood spilled out.

I set my head to Warin's.

"We'll…find you help."

I didn't know what to say. We had seen much death on this journey, but this was too close. It was the man who had plucked me from a burned-out village. The man that had raised me from a boy. The man that had saved my life and become a father to me.

"Warin…"

Tears slid from my eyes.

Warin leaned back and stared at the ceiling. He let out a deep breath.

"It's been an honor to raise you both. Two of the finest knights I've ever known."

"Warin," said Fion, his voice cracking. "Warin. Stay with us. If we can find Sacha, he might have healing."

Warin smiled.

"I feel peace, brothers." He took another deep breath. "There is much beyond this world. I know you all will win the day and make our home safe. I believe in that. My faith goes with both of you."

"And you with us," I said.

Warin smiled, his teeth red.

"I will see you all again, but I pray it is not for a long time."

He closed his eyes, and his life left him. He slumped against the altar. Me and Fion stood there for a few moments, staring at our fallen mentor, our fallen father.

My heart ached. I turned away, my stomach twisting and turning. The edges of my vision were blurry, and it felt like I was going to puke. Fion reacted before me. I heard him hurl somewhere off the side.

I tried keeping mine down. I stared at the floor, holding a hand to my face. Everything whirled around me until I felt a hand on my shoulder.

I turned around and saw Fion.

"What…do we do?" I asked.

"We keep moving," he said.

His eyes were red rimmed, and I noticed streaks through the dirt on his face where his tears had fallen.

"What more can this place take from us?" I asked. "How much more will we have to sacrifice?"

"I...I don't know."

"It's not fair!" I shouted; anger blazed through me. "If those bastards at the council had just closed the gaps. Had they not lied for so long. If...if..." I hung my head, the tears threatened to overwhelm me.

"I know, brother." Fion patted my shoulder. "I know. They could have done much to prevent this. And those that failed are not suffering the consequences."

"If I get back, I have half a mind to make war on the council," I said.

"No..." replied Fion. "You would die. If we make it out of this, you will go back to your family and live your days in peace with them. That is what you will you do. Promise me."

"Promise you?"

Fion stared at me.

"Promise me."

Fion nodded.

"I promise you."

I looked over at Warin.

"Can we at least bury him...something?"

"Where?" asked Fion. "We have no shovels. We can dig with our swords, blunting them. But this ground is hard and does not give. Decay is different in this land."

"Let's at least lay him somewhere."

"The altar," said Fion. "It is no longer tainted."

We worked quickly. Moving Warin and placing him atop the altar. We put him with his sword, his hands crossed over it. Then we took the still warm bones of Cornelius and placed them at the front of the altar.

Fion said, "We shall remember them as the two that cleansed the church."

I nodded. "Let's go. I don't know how long we have left in this world, but let's make the most of it. Give a chance to those back home."

Fion nodded.

We left the altar and our friends, and headed into the darkness.

Chapter 34

I looked up at the sky and saw the cracks were almost closed. This should have filled me with joy. Instead, I was numb. Warin's death weighed on me.

I thought of all the death, and speaking truthfully, if it were not for Josephine and Erwin, then I would not think Warin's death was worth it.

Not that I thought it was anyways.

I would gladly trade Warin's life for the life of every council member, of all the city, and the countryside. They were unknown faces while Warin was that of my father. The man took up in his stead when the demons slew my real one.

The man that had guided me, protected me, loved me, and helped to shape me into who I was. The man whose training had kept me alive in this land, the man whose sacrifice had preserved me this far.

I could never repay him.

And I just wanted him back.

I looked at Fion. We had worked our way out of the castle and wandered close to a strange, endless sea. We walked along a rocky beach, unsure where to go.

Fion stared at the water, still reeling from Warin's loss the same as I was. I looked out at the sea. At the unnatural swirl of purple. The sea looked more like shattered glass than water. None of us had dared touch it.

Who knows what darkness it contains? Far across the sea was a parody of a setting sun. We could not see it from anywhere else, yet here, from this view, was a sun of some sort.

I shook my head and turned to Fion. Though the cracks had weakened, they still existed, which meant our mourning would end fast.

"Alaric," Fion spoke.

I walked next to him and stared at the same spot in the glassy sea he did.

"Yes, brother?" I asked.

"He's gone."

"He is."

Fion nodded. "I…I knew this journey was perilous. I just…I don't know. Losing Warin was not something I expected. I thought the entire company could be wiped out, including me and you, and somehow, he would still be standing."

"I had the same thought," I said. "I have never seen that man fall…"

His still form on the altar flashed in my mind.

"I…still have trouble believing it," I finished.

"I don't." Fion sniffed, then cleared his throat. "I don't want to go back to a world without him, without you. He is gone and if you follow, then I am just as home wandering through these wastes as returning."

"You have family."

"Not like this. Not like you and Warin. I have those that birthed me, but you two have been my family. Even more than the other knights. You brought me into the fold, and I do not want to leave."

"I am here, Fion." I stepped forward and clamped my hand on his shoulder.

"But for how long? Who can predict this world? Who can predict what lies around the next corner? Some shuffling monstrosity that shall snuff us all out?"

"We cannot know."

"No!" Fion shouted and stepped back, still staring at the sea. "We cannot know and so we must fear."

"There are other reactions to the unknown."

"All of them foolish."

I sighed and looked down. I felt what Fion felt, but I could not let that get the best of us.

"What would Warin have done?"

"Warin is dead."

"We are knights, Fion. We must hold ourselves together."

Fion spun, stared at me, his eyes wide.

"We are dead men. Wandering through a land of the damned, every step brings us closer to our doom."

I thrust a finger at the sky. "You see those cracks?" I asked. "They have shortened since we arrived. Through our action, we have struck back."

We stared at each other for a moment.

I slammed a fist against my chest. "We did that. Us humans with swords, holiness, and magic. Humans with will and beating hearts. We changed this."

"And yet it's not enough."

"Not yet."

"It never will be."

Fion fell to his knees. I slumped down with him. I tried to keep his eyes, but he stared at the ground.

"How long can we prevent this? How long before the cracks reopen? Eventually, this world conquers our own, Alaric. Eventually, we all fall to this."

"We can keep it back."

"It's not worth it. Better to fall into quiet oblivion."

"Never." I swatted the air in front of me. "Never, we fight, we rage against this. We defend that which we love."

"And it brings us nothing."

I slapped Fion. The blow surprised me as much as it did him. I pointed my finger at his face.

"Fion, my dearest brother, shut up and listen to me."

We locked eyes.

"There is hope. Dammit. There is hope. So long as we fight, so long…"

I realized what I was about to say, and it scared me.

"So long as we wield steel that cuts and possess a heart willing to spill blood, there is a chance. Through will, through fighting, we can preserve love, we can preserve life."

Fion shook his head. "Who are you?"

"I don't know."

Fion took a deep breath.

"Thank you…for the slap."

I nodded. "Of course."

"I will do the same should the need arise." A sliver of a smile crossed Fion's face, and it warmed my heart.

"Of course."

I looked around.

"One more demon and we shall be free."

"How do we get back?"

I stood up and offered Fion a hand. He took it. I leaned back, yanking my brother up.

"I don't know, but we shall find a way."

Fion stared at me for a moment.

"What?" I asked.

"I wish I had your faith."

"Don't be too hasty," I said. "It may be the death of us."

Chapter 35

We wandered along the glassy shore. To our left was a steep cliff that leveled out ahead of us. It was strange to hear the ebb and flow of the waves, but not the cry of gulls, nor any sound of a normal world.

Ahead of us was a turn on the beach. Fion walked a few paces past me. It had been a while since we last spoke. We came to the lower part of the cliff where the beach rounded. We started around a tight corridor when I heard a familiar sound.

The jingling of armor.

I reached forward and grabbed Fion's shoulder.

"Do you hear that?" I asked.

Fion nodded.

"So I am not mad then," I replied.

Fion chuckled. "Perhaps we're both mad."

We waited and heard the sound again.

"There is it," I said.

"It's just up ahead, around the bend," said Fion.

"You think it's Alexei?"

"I doubt it," replied Fion. "Likely some fresh horror that'll do us in."

I hesitated.

The jingling armor got closer.

"Maybe we should head back," said Fion. "It will be safer."

I looked back along the slim corridor we had walked.

"And go where?" I asked. "Whoever is coming can see us for a great distance. And we have nowhere to hide, nowhere to lie in wait." I turned towards the bend and stepped in front of Fion.

"Come."

Fion sighed. "I suppose if this is where is it to end...it could be worse."

We stepped around the bend and stared down a corridor like the one we had walked up. On one side was a steep cliff and the other the sea of glass. But that was not what caught my eye. What caught my eye was the figure standing a stone's throw from us.

He wore black armor and stood two heads taller than me or Fion. He had a sword strapped to his side. He wore a helm with a pointed snout. Something about the figure looked familiar to me. I'd swear it was Aldin the Unchallenged except for the tarnished state of his armor.

But there was something else.

The figure radiated power and darkness unlike anything we had yet encountered. Fion took a step back.

"This is not our fight," he said. "This is not one we shall win."

The knight reached up and retrieved his sword. He drew the blade and advanced on us.

"It's just a knight. Just a man," I said. "It's two against one. We can easily beat him and rid the land of one more darkness."

"Alaric...is it him?"

"Impossible. Come." I stepped forward and met the knight.

We both swung and our swords connected. The power coursing through my blade surprised me. Immediately, I realized I was outmatched. The knight must have seen the panic in my eyes because he paced forward, swinging in a flurry of blows.

I defended best I could, but each blow threatened to knock my sword from my hand. The knight relented. Fion's sword flashed as he drove the demon back. The knight fell back under the onslaught.

I ran forward. We both attacked the knight with ferocity. The knight defended our blows, but we gained ground. The knight stopped, and I saw an opening. I thrust my sword at the knight's neck.

The knight turned and deflected the blow, his own sword already countering. The blade flashed for me and knew I was about to die or suffer a grievous wound. Then another flash of steel and Fion deflected the blow.

The knight stepped back, and we stood facing the knight, our swords up and his at the ready. Me and Fion spread out to either side, to get as much of an angle as we could on the creature in the cramped space.

The knight lashed out. Fion fell, and I stood in his place. With a few blows, the knight forced me into the glassy water. My foot hit, and I knew something was wrong with the water. It resisted my movement, almost knocked me down.

I felt a burning along my ankle and pivoted to get out of the water. But my pivot was hasty and put me off balance. The knight crashed in and sent me to my back. Fion was up and at the knight, keeping me from death once more.

I got to my feet just in time to see Fion nearly tossed into the ocean. I ran forward and thrust. My sword smashed into the knight's chest, knocking him back a few paces. I grabbed Fion to steady him.

"Run!" I shouted.

We turned, tucked our swords away, and ran. We pounded down the beach, without either of us turning to see if the knight followed.

We ran and ran and ran.

Until we collapsed from our exhaustion.

Chapter 36

I leaned against the stump of a thick tree, my body heaving. I looked over and saw Fion on his knees, using his hands for support. He looked nearly sick. I glanced behind us, half expecting the dread knight to be on our tail.

But I saw nothing.

I looked around. We were back in a wooded area. Ahead of us was a rather pleasant country bridge spanning a shallow stream below it. The fog was sparse here and I could see down the lane we traveled.

Further ahead I spotted amber fields and a path that cut through them. Beyond, there was a rise that blocked the rest of the land from view.

I leaned against the tree and sank down it until I rested. I closed my eyes and tried to get my breath back. Never in my life had I run so far or so fast. It was like something had possessed me and, upon leaving me, had left my body broken.

I turned to Fion; my back pressed against the tree trunk. He coughed and looked up; his body convulsed from his deep breaths. I looked down the path we had traveled. It was empty, empty like so much of this land was.

A land of emptiness and horror.

Fion got to his knees and sighed. He looked over at me.

"I thought I was going to choke up my heart there for a moment."

"I felt the same," I replied.

Fion stretched out a hand towards the road in front of us. He held it there for a moment, then dropped it, too tired to sustain the effort. He shook his head.

"What fresh horror lies ahead?"

"I…I don't know," I replied. "Hopefully, something we can manage."

Fion shook his head. "We have yet to meet a task that the two of us can handle here."

"We will prevail," I said.

I didn't believe it, but I couldn't say otherwise. Fion nodded.

"Of course."

He chuckled, and I joined in. Our chuckles turned to a fit of laughter. Though there was little humor in our situation. We sat there and laughed for a few minutes, the laughter doing nothing to aid our spent lungs.

The laughter subsided, and we sat; stared at one another. He shook his head.

"We've gone mad, haven't we?"

"Not yet," I replied. "Otherwise, you would not ask that question."

"Ah, so just you then?" replied Fion.

I smiled and then forced myself to my feet.

"We should get moving."

Fion nodded. "Right, we should do many things. That doesn't mean I want to."

I walked over and held out my hand to him. He grabbed it and I helped him up. He looked at me, fear crossed his face.

"I fear the journey ahead."

I grabbed his shoulder.

"I know. I know…"

He looked at me.

"We'll bear it together," I said.

"Ah." Fion smiled and nodded. "Well, now, all my fears are quelled."

I gave him a push and laughed. "Come on now."

We walked across the bridge and into the amber fields. The path winded around small hills that dotted the landscape. I half expected to see a small farmhouse around every bend. The sky overhead was overcast but gave enough light to see the world.

"A rather pleasant part of this land," I said.

Fion nodded. "It is. I can only imagine the horrors it contains to make up for it."

I shook my head.

"Ever on the bright side?"

Fion laughed then frowned. "You know he loved you."

Fion's words stopped me. I turned, Fion stared at me. A warmth to his face.

"You were dear to him," said Fion.

"I…I know." I replied. My eyes misted. "What…what made you say that?"

"I want you to know."

I sniffed and nodded. "He loved you too."

"I know," replied Fion.

We continued our walk. A weight was over my heart and growing. Every step in this land filled me with frustration.

"If we were to ever get back," said Fion. "I'd have a word, more than a word, with the council."

"Ha!" I nodded. "I have a blade for them, not words."

"That's what I meant," said Fion. "Bastards, all of them."

"What happened to ignoring the council and living the quiet life?"

Fion kicked a stone that scudded down the dirt path ahead of us. He shrugged.

A bellow sent us both scurrying off to the side of the trail with our swords drawn. We waited and heard the bellow again. It came from around a bend in front of us.

"Damn this," said Fion. "What now?"

His voice was loud and filled with annoyance.

"Damn hiding," I said, striding out onto the path. "Whatever it is. Let's meet it."

"Aye," said Fion, stepping onto the road.

Swords drawn, standing shoulder to shoulder, we advanced around the bend.

The path ended. Beyond it was a wide circular clearing, the hills of amber grain surrounded it. In the center of the clearing was a demon. Heavily armored like the rest, it walked on four hooved feet. It snorted and shook its head.

Two great horns jutted from atop its head. It had two glowing red eyes. A weighted tail dragged behind it with spiked ball at the end like a mace.

The creature turned to us and snorted. It was not larger than a bull back home, but there was a darkness that cascaded off it.

"Alright," said Fion. "Let's be done with. Let's gut this monster and see where that takes us."

"Fion, we—"

"To arms!" Fion rushed the bull.

I charged after him. It felt good, losing myself in the moment. Breaking free of the shackles of death and worry. To live in the moment through violence. The creature reared back on its back hooves. Along its belly was a maw filled with gaping teeth.

"Come on now," said Fion, dancing around to the creature's right as I circled to its left.

The creature landed and charged at Fion. Fion rolled away and came to his feet as the creature circled around the perimeter of the circle.

"Come out!" shouted Fion, following the creature.

"Do not follow, Fion," I said. "Be wise."

"We give it space and it'll charge. Come on."

Fion ran towards the creature.

He had a point.

I ran at the creature as well. It pivoted towards us and lowered its horn. Me and Fion came from either side. The creature kicked out its hind legs towards me. I swung, my sword bit across the creature's hoof.

Fion swung, and I heard a wet sloshing sound. I backed away and saw Fion had lodged his sword into the creature's head. He withdrew the sword, and the creature slumped over. I pounced and drove my sword deep into the creature's head, ensuring it was dead.

I pulled my sword free, the black ichor dripped off. We looked up at the cracks and saw a shudder. The cracks drifted a little closer together. If we had not been watching, we would not have been able to tell the difference.

But the cracks had changed.

Fion gave a whoop. I looked down, and he slammed into me, wrapped his arms around me.

"By hell we did it," said Fion. "We did it. Just me and you. We slew one of the bastards and look!" Fion pointed to the sky. "It made a difference."

I nodded.

"Twelve more and the cracks will be closed," I said.

Fion slapped me on the shoulder. "When did you become the dreary one?"

I laughed. I looked at the monster.

"That wasn't too bad."

"No," said Fion, shaking his head with vigor. "Not at all. We just have to face these monsters. They use our fear to find openings, to strike. If we take the fight to them, maybe we'll have a chance."

"Maybe," I said.

Fion sat down, shaking his head.

"Maybe there is a chance."

"Maybe," I said.

Fion looked up at the sky.

"You think he can see us?" he asked.

"I don't know," I replied.

"I hope so." Fion held up a fist. "We'll make the most of it, Warin," he said.

I smiled. It was nice to see Fion like this. A rare form for him. I looked at the slain monster. Fion had a point, that was not as hard as I thought it would be. We went on the offensive and caught the creature off guard.

And we slew him.

I held out my hand towards Fion.

"We did him proud," I said.

It felt good. Fion grabbed my hand, and I yanked him up.

"Now let's move. There are plenty more opportunities to do him proud in this land."

We turned and ventured over the hill ahead of us.

Perhaps he was right.

Perhaps there was a chance.

Maybe I would see Josephine and Erwin again.

Maybe there was still a chance for hope.

Chapter 37

For the first time since I had arrived in this land, I felt close to elation. Me and Fion marched over the hills, the death of the demon buoyed each of our steps. Soon the hilly fields of amber gave way to more flat land filled with ruins.

Pockets of fog gathered here and there, giving the land an ominous look. The grass was a lush green and, in the distance, I could see the beginning of another forest. We walked over a slight incline and looked down.

There, amid a circle of stones, were two familiar figures. Sacha sat with his arms crossed, his back against a stone, while Alexei stood over him. Alexei leaned down and tried to coax his brother up.

Sacha looked up and saw us. He perked up and reached a hand up, snagging his brother's forearm. Alexei followed his brother's gaze, placing one hand on his sword. Upon seeing us, he released the sword and gave a cry.

We rushed down to them and them to us. We slammed into each other, embracing like old friends.

"What happened?" asked Alexei.

I looked at the giant noblemen and saw he had fresh scars and bruises. One of his eyes had a gash that nearly sealed it shut.

"What happened to you?" I asked. "You were in the room with us and then nothing."

Alexei explained they had ended up outside the castle before the darkness had cleared. They waited, but the darkness did not relent. Alexei tried to enter again, but Sacha forbade it. They thought us dead and continued on. A hooded warrior ambushed them on the road. The warrior pursued them to the fields where they bested it. Then they came here to rest.

I told them of Cornelius and Warin. Both were pained to hear of their fate. In the end, we both looked up and stared at the cracks above.

"We won't forget their sacrifice," said Alexei. "We shall forget no one who has died on this damned quest. We will see it through to the end."

Alexei looked around at each of us.

The man's confidence was a great envy of mine. It seemed to beam out from his eyes. Sacha looked up at his brother, a more cautious expression on the younger's face.

"We should be moving," I said.

We ventured on, winding down the broken paths of rubble amid the ruins. We talked, sang a few songs, anything to keep out the feeling of dread that crept its way back in.

I found I looked forward to finding a demon. Even one that proved beyond our skill. Anything to stop this in-between period of waiting, anything to stop this walking around and waiting for the worst.

The path we were on led towards the forest.

Alexei was first to take the bend into the forest and stopped. He held out a hand, stopping the rest of the group.

"What do you see?" asked Sacha.

Alexei placed a hand on his sword.

"A…a knight, it seems."

Fear pulsed through my chest. I walked around Alexei and stared into the forest. Down the path there was a glade where an old altar sat. Leaning against it was the knight from the beach. I grabbed Alexei's shoulder and pulled him back.

Alexei looked at me, annoyed.

"What is this?" he asked.

"We do not want to fight that knight," I said.

"The knight is back?" asked Fion.

I nodded.

"You know this knight?" asked Alexei.

"We faced him," said Fion. "And he nearly undid us both."

Alexei glanced around. "But now we have four as opposed to two, and the creature is alone. Surely, he is not that powerful. It is just a man, from the looks of it."

"Alexei," said Sacha. "You know better than to trust your eyes in this land. If the knight were just a man, he would not have lived this long and he would not have attacked our friends here."

"I realize that," replied Alexei. "We have four and he is one. This is a chance to slay another demon, no? A chance to seal this up and return home?"

I looked at the knight. The same menace and power dripped off the creature, even more than before. I shook my head.

"It is a significant risk," I said.

"So is everything in this land," replied Alexei. "Every step could be the end. So what more is this? He is alone. Let us face him. Let us be done with it." Alexei pounded his chest. "We are able. Such a small thing shall not undo us."

"Alexei, we should listen to them. They have faced this being, we have not," said Sacha.

The more I thought about it, the more I thought we might slay this knight. I turned to Fion. I could tell he thought otherwise.

"No, Alaric," he said.

"Why not?" I asked.

"We barely escaped with our lives. He was completely unharmed by us. We are lucky to still be alive."

"But there are four of us now," I said.

Fion looked at me like I had grown another head.

"Do you so easily forget?" he asked.

"Four, twice two."

Fion smacked a hand to his head. "I can do the addition, friend. This one is too risky. Let's find another bull or something."

"Hmm." Alexei seemed deep in thought. "We may not get another chance, and look, he lies there alone. Sacha, you can fire a bolt at him, and we could lie along the path in ambush."

"You want me to stand out there alone?" asked Sacha.

Alexei shrugged. "I will be by you. I will leap out and stop him."

Alexei seemed to stand taller at the suggestion.

I held up a hand. "This will be no simple task. We cannot leave anyone alone for long."

The knight stood; his armor creaked as he did. We shuffled to the side of the path, staring at the creature. It turned to where we had stood. The menace coming off the creature was palpable.

It turned, marching deeper into the forest. When it had gone from view, I realized we would not have survived that battle. I stood up and looked over at Alexei and Sacha.

"There is a deep darkness to that creature," said Alexei.

"We are best to leave it alone," said Fion. "There are only four of us."

"But we must keep fighting," said Alexei.

"And we will," I replied.

"It was for the best that it left," said Sacha.

"We could have taken it," replied Alexei.

"You overestimate yourself, brother," said Sacha.

Alexei frowned and seemed hurt by the statement. "I can hold my own, brother."

"I never said you could not."

I held up my hands again. "We should keep moving."

The brothers stared at each for a moment, then relented.

"Yes," said Alexei. "That would be wise."

Chapter 38

Alexei seemed disturbed. He wore an uncharacteristic frown and seemed annoyed by everything around him.

"I assure you," I said. "We made the right choice."

Alexei looked at me, his face softening. "I know…"

"But something bothers you?"

Alexei looked ahead of us. Up a cobbled path that winded through ruins. He shrugged.

"I don't like…not being able to face a challenge. It makes me feel…less."

"Less?"

He nodded.

"Half of wisdom is knowing when you're outmatched," said Fion from the rear of the pack.

Sacha laughed. "That's the thing with Alexei. He thinks himself unmatched."

"That is not true." Alexei turned to Sacha, a moment of annoyance on his face. "That is not true. I think I am able, yes, strong even. But I know I am not invincible. I'd just rather have fought the knight, killed him, and been done with this whole mess. But I agree with our knight's judgement. I trust them."

"I bet there's a way to defeat that knight," said Sacha. "We just haven't thought of it yet."

"We haven't thought of many things," said Alexei.

"I think I could figure it out, if given time," replied Sacha.

"With time, many things are possible," said Alexei.

We crested over a rise and saw a wide field before us. Knee high grass swayed in a light wind. Perched among the grass were many hooded forms. At first I thought them to be a smattering of scarecrows, but upon closer inspection I saw they moved.

I counted a dozen of them. One looked up. His pale features hidden underneath his hood. The creatures looked close to human, though I knew in this world that was impossible.

The creature that noticed me turned to me in full. He wore a long tattered black robe. Pale hands hung at his side. He glided across the grass, moving closer to us.

"Looks like we have a fight," I said.

I looked from creature to creature. One by one, they noticed us. Three glided across the grass. I drew my sword. I was eager for the fight. Eager for something to lose myself in, eager for something to bring me closer to them.

I charged the first creature.

"Alaric!" shouted Fion.

We locked eyes, and the battle began. I closed the distance to the creature and brought my sword back to swing. The creature threw out both hands. Arcs of black energy shot out, followed by pain along my side and body.

The energy tossed me back. I rolled along the ground, looked up and saw black lightning shoot from the creature's hands. A blue bolt slammed into the creature's chest and it let out a screech, falling to the earth.

The other creatures converged on us. I threw myself into the fight. Two creatures came at me from either side. One threw out its hands and I rolled. I felt the disturbance of the dark energy behind me.

I got to my feet and thrust my sword, stabbing through the chest of one creature. It went down amid shrieking wails. Another neared and attacked. It threw me to the ground, pain radiated through my body.

I stumbled to my feet in time to see Alexei hack the creature that had attacked me in two. The warrior seemed less affected by the dark energy than me. I spotted Fion recovering from a roll, his face twisted in pain.

Another blue bolt blazed by as I charged a creature. The creature was focused on Fion and died with my sword through the back of its head. I disengaged and sought the next creature. It shot its hands out as I moved. I put my sword between the creature and me. The blade attracted the energy, lessening its effect. The impact knocked me back a few paces, but it was far less forceful than a direct blow.

I closed the distance and swung. My blade cut through the creature's midsection. It screeched and fell to the earth. I glanced around. Alexei dispatched the last of the creatures. I heard a rumble above me and looked up.

The gap was closing. I gasped, as it looked like the gap would seal shut for a moment. It stayed open just a hair. I looked at Alexei and laughed.

"That…that almost did it," I said.

Alexei smiled. "We will prevail. What did I say?"

I nodded and looked at Fion. Even he had a smile.

"Look at that," I said, thrusting my hand at the cracks. "Twelve minor demons and the crack is almost closed."

"Now we need to figure out how to get out of here," said Fion.

I laughed and turned to Sacha. I grabbed his shoulder and squeezed.

"Sacha, what do you think?" I asked.

Sacha stared up at the cracks.

"We're so close."

"Let's not risk anything else," I said. "Let's find weak creatures. Another dozen of them and we will seal the cracks. We need to think of how we will get home."

"The cartographer spoke of that," said Alexei. "Though truth be told, I did not always listen when he spoke. Sacha, do you remember?"

"Bits and pieces," said Sacha. "But I can put it together. I can get us out of here."

"Good," said Alexei and I in unison.

"We have to go back towards the king…I think," said Sacha. "I'll remember."

"That fool didn't know what he spoke of," said Fion. "He could barely stand up straight, much less lead us out of here."

"He's the only one that made it back," I said. "He knew something."

Fion sighed and shook his head.

"We'll find the way out," I said. "I promise."

Chapter 39

We marched up a grassy peninsula that rose to a crest. I rested my sword on my shoulder. A distant sun gave light to the countryside and burned away most of the fog. It was nice. I leaned back and breathed in the soft wind that billowed through.

Alexei walked ahead of me. He paused a top a rocky outcrop and looked at the land below.

"The ocean," he said. "Or something akin to it."

I walked up and stood next to him. We looked over the glassy ocean I had seen before.

"This again," said Fion.

"You've been here?" asked Alexei. "To the ocean?"

"It's where we first met the knight," I said. "And it's not water. I don't know what it is, but it'll burn through your armor."

Alexei shuddered.

"One more tainted thing."

"I think it's beautiful in a way," said Sacha.

I looked over and he seemed mesmerized by the ocean.

"I wonder if it has the same effect on the creatures as it had on you," asked Sacha.

I shrugged. "I would not know."

"What are you going to do when you see father again?"

Sacha spoke, and we all turned to him. He stared at the ocean, the wind caught his hair and blew it. He looked over at Alexei, a look of contentment on his face.

"What…what am I going to do?" asked Alexei.

Sacha nodded. "Yes, when you see father."

Alexei looked uncomfortable. He looked out at the ocean.

"Well…I…" Alexei cleared his throat. "I'm not sure yet. What, what are you going to do?"

"I'm not sure," said Sacha. "See mother. Eat one of her cakes. Take father for a hunt through the countryside. I think I'll finish that painting."

"Finish the painting?" asked Alexei, turning to his brother in full. "Now? Really?"

Sacha nodded, the smile never left his face.

"I think it's time. I just never knew what was right, but now…now I think I do."

Alexei nodded. "Now that you mention it, I think I will take father for a ride. Maybe mother too if it's not too strenuous. I think…I think I shall propose to Brunhilde. I think she's waited long enough, and I've frolicked about more than anyone should stand."

Alexei shook his head.

"How little I valued time. But I will make the most of it. What about you, friends?"

Alexei turned to me and Fion.

"What will you do upon your return?"

Fion scoffed and turned away. I stared at Alexei, at those honest eyes boring into my own. I cleared my throat and stared at the ocean. It was easier staring at the glassy depths than answering that question.

"I don't know," I said.

"You don't?" asked Alexei.

"Oh, you do, Alaric," said Sascha.

When I looked over, Sacha had an eager look to him. "I know you do. I can tell you have a purpose. Something deep which you fight for."

I nodded.

"Just be with Josephine and Erwin."

"That is your wife and child?" asked Alexei.

"Of course it is," said Sacha.

I nodded. "Hold them both. Watch the wind whip through the grove. Watch a thunderstorm roll in from the mountain. Be in the stillness with them."

My heart beat faster. Something stuck in my throat, made it hard to talk. I tried swallowing, but the feeling stuck. I turned away and wiped my eyes.

"We do not mean to press," said Sacha.

Fion spoke. "I want to see my mother. Sit with her by the sea, the real sea. Have her speak to me of my father again."

I turned and stared at Fion. He hung his head and pulled in his shoulders.

"We have had many discussions. Her and I. I miss sitting and talking with her. She always listened to me, to my nonsense, to my prattling on. I know I am her one source of light left in the world. I look forward to returning to that."

He looked at me.

"I looked forward to sitting beside her and letting her know that it's not all darkness. That there is goodness, good things, and hope. To let her believe that, if just for a little while."

"A blessed time, that will be," said Alexei.

Fion nodded.

We all stood in silence, all looking at the sea. We let the breeze blow and the soft sway of the wind in the grass lull us to another place and time. For a moment, we were all with our loved ones and far away from this damned land and our damned quest.

"We have company," said Fion.

I looked up through bleary eyes and saw a figure stood at the bottom of the plateau. A familiar figure that made my hair stand on end. The dark knight.

"What is it you want from us?" I called down to him.

He stared, but there was no answer.

"It appears we cannot avoid destiny," said Alexei, walking to the fore of the group.

The dark knight watched us. His sword was out. He made no move to advance. He turned his head, taking each one of us in.

I stepped next to Alexei.

"This creature meets its death and sends us home," said Alexei. "Let's give it what it desires."

I held out my hand.

"Peace, Alexei, we must be wise about this. That creature is no fool. We cannot underestimate it."

"And we will not," replied Alexei. "But we will slay it."

The wind died down until the only sound was the four of us breathing. It was then I heard the knight breathe. It sounded human. The pitch of his helm gave it a strange metallic hue, but it felt human.

"Let's finish this," said Fion.

Fion took a step towards the knight. The knight brought up his sword and marched towards us. Sacha charged.

"Sacha, hold," said Alexei. "Fight as one."

A blue pulse glowed at the end of Sacha's drawn rapier.

"I must strike first," he called back.

The knight closed with Sacha. Sacha thrust his sword forward. The blade struck true. There was a flash of blue energy. Sacha fell back and the knight staggered.

"Damn," cried Sacha.

The knight batted aside Sacha's follow up strike and reached a hand forward, snatching Sacha's neck. There was a crunch, and the knight tossed Sacha's limp form to the ground.

Alexei let out an animal bellow and charged. He screamed his brother's name as he clashed with the knight.

"Aid him!" I shouted.

The knight and Alexei met amid a flurry of blows. The knight drove Alexei up the plateau. Me and Fion rushed to the sides, coming at the knight from behind. The knight whirled on us. He turned Fion's blow with his armor and caught mine on his sword.

The knight worked in a flash, countering, defending all three of us. It seemed the more of us there were, the more we attacked, the better the dark knight fared. We worked ourselves into a frenzy, launched everything we had at the monster.

The knight continued to drive us up the hill, towards the edge of the plateau. We disengaged and took a step back from the knight, the three of us side by side.

"Sacha. Sacha," said Alexei.

"Hold," I said.

The knight advanced on us. I lashed out, and the knight knocked aside my blow. Alexei was next to attack, a mighty overhand blow that would have shattered most men. The knight took the blow on his sword and diverted it.

Then Fion's sword crashed against the knight's head. The knight took two steps back and attacked. I thrust with all my might. My sword crashed against the knight's arm. The knight ripped his arm back and for a second, I thought I had struck true and pierced the flesh underneath.

Alexei was next and drove his blade up under the knight's shoulder armor. I heard a crunch and knew Alexei had struck. The knight lashed out with his sword. He nearly took my head. He turned and caught Alexei with a forearm to the jaw.

I watched Alexei's eyes roll into the back of his head as he dropped his sword and fell to the ground like an axed tree.

The knight advanced on me and Fion, driving us back to the plateau's edge. I knew what the creature's designs were. He wanted to throw one of us into the ocean beyond. I wanted to quell his advance, but there was nothing I could do.

We wilted under the assault. Nearly sprinting back from the knight's ferocity. During a moment of weakness, the knight knocked my sword from my hands. I watched in shock as my sword flew from my grasp. The knight thrust and I leapt back.

The sword tip scrapped along my leg armor and sliced part of my thigh. I fell from the momentum of the sprawl and looked up to see a boot crashing towards my face. I rolled, and the knight missed.

I went to get up when a knee to the ribs slammed me against the earth. I looked up, expecting a death blow. Instead, Fion tangled with the knight, his sword in the grass by me. The knight ripped Fion back and forth, trying to throw him.

I snatched up the sword and charged after the two whirling bodies. I cursed Fion. He led the knight to the cliff edge, tried to throw the much bigger creature.

I brought the sword up and swung for the knight's head. It connected, making a metallic ring that cut through the air. The knight threw Fion who rolled a step away from the plateau's drop. The knight snatched Fion's sword from my hand and knocked me to the ground.

I looked up as the knight brought its sword back to strike. Then Fion's forearm was around the brute's neck and he wretched back. Both knight and friend plummeted over the edge of the plateau.

It happened so quick I didn't get to call Fion's name. I scrambled to the edge of the plateau like a fool. I looked down into the sea of glass. Both bodies crashed into the ocean.

Fion's hand shot up and his face emerged. He screamed, his face peeling away. I reached my hand out to him, even though he was so far away. I slid off the cliff. As I fell forward, a firm hand grabbed my shoulder and yanked me back.

Fion dipped below the ocean and did not rise. His scream still echoed in the air and wrote itself in my heart and head.

My eyes searched the glassy sea for signs of Fion, but there were none. There would be none. He could not have survived that plunge. I searched for the knight and saw no sign of the creature.

I looked back at the cracks and saw nothing had changed. I hung my head at the edge of the plateau and let tears fall that had built for some time. Alexei sat by my side. Sacha joined up next.

I did not have time to marvel at Sacha's survival. Only at the pain of losing Fion. Only at the pain of losing those I loved.

At the realization that this land was going to take everything from us and there was nothing we could do to stop it.

Chapter 40

I felt like a ghost. Alexei and Sacha spoke, but their words were faint echoes. Twice they had pulled me back from the deadly waters. My hands burned, as did my ankles and knees.

The brothers had wrested me away and set me in a nearby forest. Alexei stood in front of me, talking with Sacha in a low voice.

"A decisive strike," said Alexei, making a chopping motion with his hand. "End it all and be done with it."

"You saw how quick things can turn," said Sacha. "A few moments ago we were four and now we are three."

"Hush. He's coming to."

I blinked and looked from one brother to the other.

"I see sanity in your eyes again," said Alexei.

I nodded. "What little there is to be had."

"I am sorry for your loss, friend," said Sacha.

"Thank you." I wiped my face. "We should get moving."

"To where?" asked Alexei.

"To the next creature." Rage built in me. "To the next damn bastard that's keeping us from our families. To the next bastard that killed our friends. To the next bastard making us go through hell."

My heartbeat thudded in my head. "Let's kill them. Just find one, I don't care what and kill them. I want to watch them die."

Alexei looked at Sacha, then back at me.

"The pain is deep, friend," he said. "I cannot imagine losing one such as him. He was a brother to you, it seemed. Were something to happen to Sacha, I know I'd feel the same way."

Alexei stepped forward. He raised a hand as if to put it on my shoulder, then retracted it.

"We will go together and wedge the cracks closed."

I nodded. "Let's go. We talked long enough."

Alexei clapped his hands. "Agreed."

"You may wish to wait a moment," said Sacha. "Let whatever storms inside you subside, so that you can see clearly or as clearly as one can."

"I see clearly," I said, wiping a tear from a blurry eye. "And I know what I want. I want to see them dead."

"Then let us go," said Alexei.

"Two skilled warriors," said Sacha. "I hope I can contribute something to this."

"Sacha, brother." Alexei slapped his brother on the back. "You are more help than you know."

Sacha smiled at his brother's words.

I stepped between the brothers.

"We should be moving."

We trekked through the forest and across the plains. The ocean disappeared behind us. I led us through twisting mazes of trees and across the ruins of long dead cities. Wherever I sensed darkness, I raced towards it.

But I could find nothing.

We dove through dark caverns and decrepit pits, but we found no demons. We saw an old fort and explored it, but there were no devils. Another mist shrouded forest turned up nothing. I came to a great overlook and glanced at the valley stretching out below. Mist clung to places here and there, but no demons were to be seen.

"Perhaps we cleared them all out?" asked Sacha.

"Impossible," I said. "The cracks would have shut, and this world contains untold legions of them."

"How do we know that?" asked Sacha. "Has anyone counted them?"

I shook my head.

"This makes little sense. We should be able to find something. It's like the land refuses to give us anything."

"Maybe it senses its weakness," said Sacha.

"Maybe we're not looking hard enough," I replied.

I looked over the same pieces of land, hoping to find something new. A dark castle, an abandoned fort, a foggy ravine, anything that could signal demons. Anything that could signal a way to get out of all of this.

"What about that king?" I asked.

I turned to the others.

"Do any of you know how to return there? Surely, he is a demon, is he not?"

"Many things," said Alexei. "But not a demon. Slaying him would not close the cracks."

"There's no way to know that," I said.

"Alexei speaks true," said Sacha. "He is no demon."

I gritted my teeth and turned back to the vista. I sank to the ground, burying my face in my hands.

"I want to go home," I said.

I felt a powerful hand on my left shoulder and a softer hand on my right. I looked up.

"I know," said Alexei.

"We all want to return home," said Sacha.

The two brothers sat on either side of me.

"And we will," said Alexei, staring out at the land.

The man still looked confident. Like all the setbacks were just temporary. That no matter what came, we'd be alright.

I leaned forward, placed my face in my hands again.

"I don't want to continue. To rove around this land until I die."

"It will not be long," said Alexei.

Sacha stood up and went to the overlook.

"This land is vast," said Sacha. "There is still so much we have not explored. We'll find more demons, of that I'm sure, and when we do, we shall slay them."

"And then go home," said Alexei.

"And then go home," repeated Sacha.

"Then where are they?" I asked. "They need to show themselves."

I looked up and was unsure of what I saw. A grey glimmer bore down on me. I don't know where the creature came from or how it crept up on us without making a sound. It was large, covered with scaled armor.

It walked upright with large, padded feet and had a great horn sticking out of the center of its snout. It bore down on me, and I knew I was dead.

I saw a flash of blue and Sacha was in front of me. But he shouldn't have been. The creature and its horn were there. I saw the horn again, sticking out of the back of Sacha as the creature lifted him off the ground.

I watched Sacha pour three bolts into the creature's neck as it carried him beyond us and down the hill. The creature crashed and Sacha rolled off. He lay there in a daze, a gaping wound in his chest squirting blood.

"No, no, no, no!" Alexei shouted and scrambled to his brother.

Everything had happened so fast, it felt like I had not blinked since speaking to Alexei. I stood up and raced over to Sacha. Alexei cradled him, shook his head as he watched blood pour from his brother's mouth.

He whispered his brother's name and shook his head.

"No, no, no. I promised mother I'd protect you. No, I promised her. Sacha, Sacha speak to me."

Sacha rolled his head over and looked up at his brother.

"I did it," he said.

"You did what?" asked Alexei.

Sacha's head rolled back, and he spoke no more.

"You did what, brother? Tell me, what did you do?" Alexei held Sacha up to him.

Sacha looked even smaller in the massive arms of his brother.

"Sacha, Sacha, please say something," said Alexei.

I went and squatted by Alexei. It took a while, but eventually he stopped saying his brother's name. He sat there with his slain brother in his arms. He stared at his brother, as if what he saw wasn't real.

I waited, not saying anything.

Alexei shook his head.

"I promised."

I reached out and grabbed Alexei's shoulder.

"I know."

"I promised to keep him safe and now he's dead," Alexei sniffed. "My sweet little Sacha. My baby brother. I…"

Something changed in Alexei's eyes. As he got up, he clung to his lifeless brother. He leaned back and let out a yell that echoed through the land. He turned to me.

"I bury my brother."

I nodded.

"And then we slay them all."

I nodded.

Alexei looked down at his brother.

"I'll avenge you," he said.

He looked at me, as if seeking confirmation.

I nodded.

"We'll kill them all."

Chapter 41

My fire faded fast. This land quenched my warring side, but not in a good way. Alexei and I trekked through desolation. It seemed the further we traveled, the less likely we were to spot any demons.

Every promising overlook proved to be a dead end. Every distraught building or clouded grotto was nothing but overgrown landscapes and ruins. A thought occurred to me that chilled my bones.

What if they had all broken through?

The cracks were still open and passage possible. I did not know how long we had been here, but it had to be enough time for more groups to slip through.

What if the strongest ones had broken through and now rampaged through the countryside?

I stopped and walked to a low wall on the forested path we trekked. I sat on it. Alexei turned to me.

"What are you doing?" he asked.

I stared ahead, not answering.

Alexei walked to me. He reached down and grabbed my arm.

"Come on. We must go. I have a brother to avenge, a family name to uphold. We have the cracks to seal, now is not the time to sit. Mourn, cry, do whatever you must do, but do it later."

"What if they're already through?"

Alexei took a step back.

"What?"

"What if they're already through?" I repeated the question.

Alexei looked at the cracks and then down at me.

"What if that's why we can't find them?" I asked.

"Nonsense," said Alexei. "I refuse to believe it."

I looked at Alexei, met his eyes.

"Why? Because it's too horrible to contemplate?"

Alexei nodded. "That is exactly why."

Alexei pulled me up. I didn't fight him.

"That is why we must move. If we are too late…then we are too late. But now is not the time to think of such things. You know that, you are a soldier."

"I am. But I am also a father, a husband."

Alexei grabbed my shoulders, steadied me so he could look into my eyes.

"If the worst has happened…there is nothing you can do. But that is not what has happened. We still have a chance, we still have time. But if we sit around and doubt, then we may miss our chance to seal the cracks and save them."

I nodded. He made sense, yet my heart and my mind did not respond.

"I wish I saw a demon. Something I could face. This wandering leaves me weary," I said.

"We'll find our enemy."

"The ruins are empty. The forests, the caves, the castles are also—"

A figure stepped out from behind a broken wall across the road and started down the path. My mouth hung open. Alexei whirled with his sword.

It was a knight. A human knight. One that looked like he came from the normal world a few hours prior. His armor still shone, and the cape he wore had barely faded.

"Friend!" I reached a hand towards the knight.

Alexei's arm shot out, and he restrained me.

"Caution, Alaric," he said.

I pushed Alexei's hand down. "Do you feel darkness coming off this one?" I asked.

I pushed back the big man. "This one is a friend."

"Knight!" I waved at the knight's back.

The knight did not respond. I raced around in front of the knight and stopped short. I went to shout at him again, but my voice caught.

The knight's face was tightened. His eyes hollow. The skin had turned a brittle brown like stretched leather. The knight's lips moved, but no words came out. His lips were cracked and split. His collar bone poked up underneath his armor.

He wavered back and forth as he walked, stumbled every few steps. It surprised me I had not noticed it earlier. I took a step back and looked at Alexei. Alexei rushed up with his sword.

I held up a hand, indicated Alexei to stop. Alexei slowed and walked to me, staring at the knight.

"He's no demon," I said.

Alexei stared. "Are you sure?"

I nodded. "You feel anything? Any darkness?"

"I do not."

"And neither do I. Look at him. He was once human and not too long ago."

We took a few steps back as the poor creature shuffled down the path.

"What is he?" asked Alexei.

I stared at the knight, the markings on his armor. At the clasp that held his cape in place. It looked older than my own, but not by much.

"He's a Knight of the Order, one lost in a breach."

"A knight from a breach?" asked Alexei. "What happened to him?"

I stared at the strange creature before me. He let out a low groan that sounded sad. I reached out to him, but the knight showed no reaction.

"He's lost himself to this place," I said.

"How do we not end up this way?" asked Alexei.

I stepped aside and let the faded knight pass. I watched as he meandered down the street. At one point, he stopped and reached out his hand to a distant horizon. He let off a few low moans, then resumed his walk.

"By fighting," I said. "It's the only way forward. The only way to keep our sanity. To keep doing what we must to bring about the end of our quest."

"He lost his fight then?"

I shrugged. "I can't say. But if I had to guess, I think he lost his purpose."

Alexei nodded. "Wise. We should go, less we become like him."

"But to where?"

Alexei shrugged and held out his hand to the world. "Wherever there are demons."

Something shifted in my stomach. I would not call it a fire, but something stirred, locking into place.

"I think I know a place we can go."

Chapter 42

The waves of the glassy sea lapped against the beach below. The strange sun stood over the sea like a shepherd watching its flock. A calmness flowed through me. One I had not felt in a while.

Alexei watched the sea; his chest rose and fell to the swells.

"It's peaceful in a way," he said.

I scratched my chin, looked at the beach. I knew there was a demon that would meet us this way. A demon that if slain, would close the cracks once and for all.

"I miss my brother," said Alexei.

I looked at him.

"I know."

Alexei sighed.

"Death is not fierce now. He was the closest one to me and now he is gone. Father, mother, I love them, but it is not the same. Sacha, he understood me and now he is gone."

"I am sorry, Alexei."

Alexei shrugged.

"As am I. You came here to find the knight, yes?"

I nodded.

"He will kill us."

I nodded again.

"But you want to fight anyway. To try."

"Yes."

Alexei smiled.

"You do your brotherhood honor. You are a true knight, how I always thought of them. In the story books and when I was young and would watch them march down the streets." Alexei shook his head. "How I wanted to be one."

I laughed. "I never did. Warin saved me from a burned-out village, trained me, and that was that."

"My father said the knights would take me away from my political duties, ha!" Alexei smirked. "My duties are to my family, not some political schemes."

"You bring your family honor. I'm sure your father would be proud of you."

A light sparkled in Alexei's eye. As if I had just given him a kingdom of gold. He looked away and cleared his throat.

"Your words strike deep, friend. Though without Sacha, all victories leave me with a bitter taste."

"Then let us go," I said. "To one last battle. One last victory or defeat. Either we will join those that walked with us, or we will save those we love."

"Do you think we have a chance?" asked Alexei.

"We fight. Everything else is out of our hands."

Alexei smiled.

"It's an honor to fight with you, by your side."

"The honor is mine."

I heard twigs snap behind me. I knew he was there. Me and Alexei turned and faced our opponent. The dread knight walked out of the darkened wood. He stood, staring at us both.

"This is it, knight," I said. "Here it is decided."

I looked around at what would be our arena, a small glade that overlooked the ocean below. Large trees backed the knight, and the open air stood behind us. To our left was a broken stone wall. Me and Alexei spread out to either side. The knight readied his sword.

Alexei struck first.

He rushed forward and swung a mighty blow at the knight. The knight stepped back and blocked the blow. I rushed in and thrust for the knight's midsection. The knight twisted and knocked my blade aside.

We pivoted and turned. Alexei was on one side and the knight and me on the other. We both attacked. The knight rushed forward, knocked aside my sword and lowered his shoulder. He knocked me on my back.

I rolled up and swung, catching the knight on the side of the head. The knight stumbled and Alexei took a mighty swing. The knight dodged the blow, his head saved by a sliver of space.

The knight attacked Alexei, driving him back.

I lunged for the knight, shot my sword for behind his knee. The knight disengaged from Alexei and blocked my strike. He struck me on the side of my head with a backhand that made me dizzy.

I looked over, expecting a follow up blow, but could see nothing. The knight had cut my temple and blood seeped into my eyes, blinding me. I swiped at it as I ducked away.

Through the blood I saw Alexei grappled with the knight, his bear-like arms wrapped around the knight's own, but the knight was too powerful and broke free. He turned and buried his sword into Alexei's stomach. Alexei smashed the knight on the side of the head, sent him stumbling a few feet.

I ran forward and swung. The knight turned and caught the blow on his gauntlet. The edge of my sword swiped across the knight's face. My sword cut across his eye hole and a black ichor leaked out.

I advanced as the knight fell back. The knight blocked my first few strikes, then I feinted. The knight bit on the feint and I struck. My sword entered the knight's neck. The knight made a gurgling sound and fell a step back.

I yanked my sword free and swung. The blade glanced off the knight's pauldron and shore into his neck, wedging itself there. I stared at the knight as ichor spilled down its chest. I stepped back, and let the knight fall to its knees.

I freed my sword from the knight's neck. The knight fell forward on its hands and knees. I brought the blade up then into the back of the knight's head. The knight crashed against the ground.

I walked around the back of the knight and swung my sword down into the creature's neck. I stepped back, my sword still wedged inside the monster.

I heard clapping. I looked over and saw Alexei sat against the broken wall, his legs sprawled out before him. I noticed his skin looked grey.

"Well fought," said the warrior. "Well fought, my friend."

Alexei's face turned from one of happiness to one of horror.

I spun, expecting the knight to lurch from the grave to face me once more. Instead, my sword was in the same place, the knight still dead. It was then I heard tinkling glass.

I looked up and saw the most beautiful sight I had ever seen.

The cracks fluxed and then shattered. Like tiny bits of glass in the sky, dissipating into the night. I thrust my fist into the sky and gave a mighty cry. I turned to Alexei.

"We did it!" I shouted.

Alexei smiled a pained smile. I realized he was dying. I rushed over to him and knelt, placing my hand on his shoulder.

"I am sorry, friend," I said. "You fought bravely. I could not have done it without you."

Alexei smiled but said nothing.

"What's wrong?"

"Brother." Alexei smiled and placed a hand on my shoulder.

His smile faded, then came back.

"Brother, you saved them."

I sniffed and shook my head. "We did. All of us."

I looked at Alexei's wound. He bled.

"We have to staunch the bleeding," I said.

I glanced around, looked for something to wrap around Alexei. Tucked into the knight's side, I saw a shard of cloth. I stood up to retrieve it. I took a step forward and fell. The world around me spun.

"What…what's wrong with me?" I chuckled as I tried rising to my feet, but my body would not cooperate.

"I'm so sorry, friend," said Alexei.

"Sorry?" I asked, "What are you sorry for, brother?"

Alexei wiped a tear from his eye.

"I'm sorry."

"What…" I felt a wetness I had not felt before.

I looked down and saw a dark stain spread across my side. I tapped my hand against it and looked at my fingers. My gauntlet had blood on it, my blood.

"Well now, that's not true," I said.

I reached around and then felt intense pain. I withdrew my hand.

But that couldn't be.

I tore off my chest piece and observed the place where the knight struck. Blood pooled around it. I should have realized. I looked at Alexei, I must have looked shocked.

"I didn't know how to tell you," he said.

I grabbed the cloth from the knight and crawled over to Alexei. I used the last of my strength to press it against his chest.

"Here."

I went to wrap it around him, but my strength gave. I collapsed against the wall, shoulder to shoulder, with Alexei.

"I feel cold," said Alexei.

"As do I."

Alexei looked over and laughed.

"What are you laughing at?" I asked.

"We did it," said Alexei. "We won."

Chapter 43

The cracks bursting was one of the most beautiful things I had ever seen. Me and Alexei lay against one another, staring up at the clear sky.

"That song," said Alexei. "The one you sang in the forest, when we all reunited…do you mind singing a few verses? I would like to hear it before I go,"

I cleared my throat. "My voice is weak, brother, but I shall do my best."

I took a deep breath and sang.

Come to me in this dark hour,

With my brethren far from me,

Lead my shaking hands to virtue,

That I may be blessed with Thee.

This I'll take and stand upon it.

Upon Thine guiding light.

I'll meet the darkness, stand against it.

For the sake of that I love…

I sighed. "Sing the next part with me, brother."

"I shall," said Alexei.

Together, we threw up our voices.

Like a wisp among the shadows,

Like a sparrow far from home.

I'll stand athwart the darkness,

Knowing Your true love's hold.

Be with me in this challenge,

Don't let me face it lone.

As one, we'll meet the shadow.

As one we'll make it home.

We both slumped back, panting. Every breath became a labor.

"Want to finish it, brother?" I asked.

I looked over and saw Alexei's eyes were closed and his chest no longer rose. There was a smile on his face.

"You go to them with your head held high," I said.

I sniffed, tears streamed down my face.

"I'll take us home."

With what little voice I had left, I sang.

For I know that love is with me,

For I know the truth I hold.

A home to hold and keep me.

A love to know my very own.

A love like no other.

A love I'll find in You alone.

My vision got hazy, but with it, my mind experienced clarity. I thought of Erwin and Josephine and all I could think of was if they knew the depth of my love for them. If I had communicated it enough, if I had shown it enough.

I shifted and felt something at my side. A small pouch. The one Erwin had given me to write. I rummaged through it and withdrew charcoal and parchment. I spread out the parchment on my bloody greaves.

I worked the charcoal across the parchment. I knew I had limited time. Trying to express so much in so little.

Erwin,

I love you more than words can express, and I do not feel I showed that enough. No matter what you feel in this life, know you are loved.

I look above and I see the cracks have sealed. I look above and I know you and your mother are safe…if for a time.

My life ebbs, Erwin, but I want you to know this. To save you and her, to save the two I love most in this world. I would die a thousand deaths and consider it gain.

I am so proud of you, Erwin, and I know you will accomplish great things in your life.

I hope when you look up at the sky and you see no threat, no darkness on the horizon, you will think of me.

And know I love you…

I feel so tired now. Everything seems like its slipping away.

I hope they know I love them.

I hope when they saw the cracks break, they knew, more than anything.

I love them.

Could You Do Me A Quick Favor?

That is the end of Knights of the Blood, the first book in the Kingdom Of Ash & Sorrow series. If you enjoyed the book, could you do me a quick favor?

As an indie author I live and die by reviews. If you could click on the link below and leave me a quick and honest review. It would mean the world to me.

https://www.amazon.com/review/create-review/?ie=UTF8&channel=glance-detail&asin=B0DQ678LZF

Thank you so much!

And if you enjoyed what you read be sure to check out The Dark Rises. The first book in The Dread Lands series below.

https://www.amazon.com/Dark-Rises-Dread-Lands-Book-ebook/dp/B09V46P9X3

Thanks!

-Arthur Drake

Made in the USA
Columbia, SC
06 January 2025

49351496R00157